# Silent Thief

## Cedar River Daydreams

1 ▪ New Girl in Town
2 ▪ Trouble with a Capital "T"
3 ▪ Jennifer's Secret
4 ▪ Journey to Nowhere
5 ▪ Broken Promises
6 ▪ The Intruder
7 ▪ Silent Tears No More
8 ▪ Fill My Empty Heart
9 ▪ Yesterday's Dream
10 ▪ Tomorrow's Promise
11 ▪ Something Old, Something New
12 ▪ Vanishing Star
13 ▪ No Turning Back
14 ▪ Second Chance
15 ▪ Lost and Found
16 ▪ Unheard Voices
17 ▪ Lonely Girl
18 ▪ More Than Friends
19 ▪ Never Too Late
20 ▪ The Discovery
21 ▪ A Special Kind of Love
22 ▪ Three's a Crowd
23 ▪ Silent Thief

A08

# Silent Thief

Judy Baer

BETHANY HOUSE PUBLISHERS
MINNEAPOLIS, MINNESOTA 55438

*Silent Thief*
Judy Baer

Cover illustration by Merry DeCourcy

Library of Congress Catalog Card Number 95–30279

ISBN 1–55661–588–4



Published by Bethany House Publishers
A Ministry of Bethany Fellowship, Inc.
11300 Hampshire Avenue South
Minneapolis, Minnesota 55438

Printed in the United States of America

For Ralph Hoppe on the occasion of his retirement from teaching. Concordia College and its students will miss you. You're one of the best!

JUDY BAER received a B.A. in English and Education from Concordia College in Moorhead, Minnesota. She has had over forty novels published and is a member of the National Romance Writers of America, the Society of Children's Book Writers, and the National Federation of Press Women.

Two of her novels, *Adrienne* and *Paige*, have been prizewinning bestsellers in the Bethany House SPRINGFLOWER series (for girls 12–15). Both books have been awarded first place for juvenile fiction in the National Federation of Press Women's communications contest.

# Chapter One

Binky McNaughton stared intently into the mirror in Lexi Leighton's bedroom. She frowned and grimaced before her features settled into a full scowl of disgust. With quick, jerky motions she grasped wisps of her reddish brown hair, piled them on top of her head, and studied the effect in the mirror. The scraggly hairdo resembled a haystack. As quickly as she'd put it up, she allowed her hair to tumble back to her shoulders. The expression on her face soured even more.

Peggy Madison, who was watching Binky from across the room, rolled her eyes and turned to Lexi. "Where's your mom today? I didn't see her when we came in."

"Mom's locked herself in the studio. She's getting ready for her first solo art show."

"At the gallery downtown?" Peggy sounded impressed. "Don't they bring people from all over the country to show in that gallery?"

"It has a good reputation. That's why Mom is working so hard on her paintings. This show is her big chance."

"Does this mean your mother's going to be famous?" Binky took time away from the mirror. "If she is, I'd better get her autograph now. She probably won't want to give it to me later."

"Well, she may not be famous, but it will increase the value of her artwork. That usually happens when an artist's reputation grows. Mom's excited. She never thought she'd get this far with her art."

"Just think," Peggy said, "we *know* her. I bet she *will* be famous someday. Her work will probably hang in the biggest art galleries in the world and we'll be able to say that our best friend is her daughter."

Binky didn't respond. She was too busy looking in the mirror to pay attention to the ongoing conversation. She splayed her fingers and touched the edges of her face just next to her ears. Then she lifted the skin until it was pulled tight across the bridge of her nose.

"Oh no!" A squeak of dismay erupted from her. She leaned forward until her nose nearly touched the mirror. "A zit on the end of my nose!" She looked cross-eyed toward its tip. "Can you believed it? Do you think I should squeeze it? Don't answer that. I don't want to know. I don't want to think about it." Binky glared at her reflection and stuck out her tongue.

"I have to ask," Lexi finally weakened. "I've been watching you do goofy things to your face for the last fifteen minutes. What in the world are you doing?"

"Other than losing her mind?" Jennifer Golden was sprawled across Lexi's bed paging through magazines.

"It's time to send Binky away for a rest. She's

losing it. There's no doubt about it."

Binky ignored them to examine a minuscule roll of fat she'd found at the waistband of her jeans. "Look at this blubber." She pinched a tiny flap of skin between her fingers and shook it.

"Look at what? I don't see anything," Lexi challenged.

"I'm a mess. I have a zit on my nose, fat at my waist, unhealthy skin. My color's bad too—don't you think it's grayish? I should drink more water. That might help. Drinking water flushes the impurities from your body. One problem with drinking all that water is that I'll have to go to the bathroom all the time. And Egg always hogs the bathroom at our house. I don't know what he does in there. Homework, I think. . . ."

"Binky, you're being even weirder than usual and that's *pretty weird*," Peggy observed.

"Just look at me." Binky turned away from the mirror and spread her hands wide.

"You're the same as always," Jennifer said.

Binky's eyes filled with tears. "I know. Isn't it awful?" She sank onto the edge of Lexi's bed, her shoulders drooping. She looked disconsolate. "I look terrible. I didn't realize what bad shape I was in until I visited Harry at college."

"So that's what this is all about," Peggy crowed. "Harry."

"No, it's not about Harry. It's about me. While I was on campus, everywhere I went I saw beautiful girls. Blondes, brunettes, redheads. Tall ones, short ones. All of them gorgeous. They looked so sophisticated and put together and . . . healthy. When I look in the mirror, I don't like what I see."

"Binky, you're perfectly good-looking and you know it." Lexi tried to sound reassuring.

"There's more to this than just seeing a bunch of beautiful girls on Harry's college campus," Jennifer muttered. "What's the *real* problem here?"

"I can't compete," Binky said in a tiny voice. "There's *no way* I can compete for Harry's attention with all those beautiful girls around. I'm surprised he calls or writes to me at all. Why should he? Every one of the girls I met was spectacular. They all looked as though they'd been working out at a gym or in-line skating six hours a day. I look so . . . " Binky searched for a word that would describe her, "Blah!"

"Binky, you look fine," Peggy said.

"No, I don't. You're saying that because you're my friend and you think you *have* to say it.

"I need a new look," Binky continued. "Something that will keep Harry interested in me. We hardly ever get to see each other and he's with those beautiful girls every single day. There has to be something about me that's special, that will keep me in his mind even when we're apart."

Jennifer snorted loudly. "Harry *has* to be interested in you, Binky. No one ever knows what you're going to do next. You're the perfect mystery woman."

"She's right," Peggy added. "Personality plus, Binky. That's you. Why would Harry *want* any other girl when he can have you?"

Binky refused to be convinced. She picked up a magazine. "Magazines always have self-improvement programs in them, don't they?" she mused. "*That*'s what I need! I'm going to start a self-improvement program. 'Firm and Tone Your Thighs in Twenty Minutes a Day.' " Binky propped the magazine open on the floor next to her. "And here's an article telling me how to have glowing skin in only fifteen minutes a day. I can do that. 'Walk Your Way to Good Health in an Hour a Day.' That's a good one."

"Wait a minute," Jennifer said. "If you spend twenty minutes on your thighs, an hour walking, fifteen minutes on your face, and all the other things you're probably planning, there won't be any hours in the day to go to school or see your friends. Be realistic!"

"But I have to do *something*. It's the only way I can hang on to Harry."

"It's the only way you *think* you can hang on to Harry," Lexi pointed out. "Has Harry said anything negative about your looks?"

"Of course not. He's too nice to do anything like that."

"Maybe he hasn't said anything because he knows you're fine just the way you are."

Binky wouldn't buy it. "I need a new look and I'm going to get one. I've been thinking about this for a long time. Now it's time to start."

Although Binky was prone to fits of enthusiasm, she usually lost interest in projects quickly. This time, however, she sounded serious. She and Harry Cramer had dated for a long time. If she thought there was something jeopardizing their relationship, Binky would do everything in her power to change it.

"What, exactly, are you planning?"

"Do you *really* want to hear about my self-improvement program, or are you just going to laugh at me?" Binky asked suspiciously.

"We won't laugh. We promise." As she spoke, Lexi gave Jennifer a warning stare. Jennifer had a tendency to blurt out what was on her mind, whether it was complimentary or not.

"All right, here goes." Binky pulled a tattered piece of paper out of the pocket of her jeans. "I've got a list."

Jennifer's eyebrows shot upward until they were hidden beneath her blond bangs. "A list?"

"Yes, my self-improvement list. I don't know why using this for a self-improvement program didn't occur to me before." Binky studied the page intently. "I've been compiling it ever since I got back from my visit with Harry.

"First of all, I'm not going to skip any more meals, especially not breakfast. I read that it makes your body switch into starvation mode. It's much better to eat three meals a day."

"Binky, you *never* skip a meal," Peggy pointed out. "You eat meals even when there aren't any meals to be eaten!"

"I'm also going to quit snacking. Junk food isn't good for your body. No more fat, no more salt. . . ."

"No more taste, no more flavor," Jennifer added.

"I'll just have to learn to like it," Binky said importantly.

"I read about an effective diet with only one rule to follow," Peggy offered. "If it tastes good, spit it out. If it tastes bad, swallow."

Binky gave her friend a disgusted look. "Do you want to hear the rest of my list or not?"

"I wouldn't miss it for the world."

"I'm not going to smoke."

"That shouldn't be too hard, Binky. You don't do that anyway."

"I know. And I'm never going to. It makes your skin gross, your lungs polluted, your breath bad, and your clothes stink. Besides that, if you smoke for a long time you get these little tiny cracky lines around your mouth that make you look about a thousand years old."

"Good. What else?"

"I'm going to floss my teeth every day."

"The dentists of America salute you."

"I may not be as beautiful as some of those girls on Harry's campus, but I'm going to have the best teeth. And I'm not going to drink soda anymore either . . . just water. Do you know that carbonation is hard on the calcium in your bones?"

"Thanks so much for sharing," Jennifer said. "I think I'm getting sick to my stomach."

"And I'm going to start walking every day . . . miles and miles."

"Isn't that overly ambitious?" Lexi asked doubtfully.

"Maybe I'll start with one mile. Egg can drive me to the mall and I'll walk in there."

"If you're going to have Egg drive you to the mall so you can walk, wouldn't it be simpler just to *walk* to the mall yourself?"

"I never thought of that."

"What would you do without me?" Jennifer stared helplessly at her friend.

"I'm also going to have a facial as soon as I save up enough money," Binky continued. "And I'm going to learn how to wear clothes so I don't always look like I shop at a thrift store."

"But you *do* shop at thrift stores, Binky."

She ignored the comment. "I'm going to save my money. That way, the next time I see Harry I can have a whole new wardrobe and really impress him. And I'm going to start reading books, newspapers—everything I can get my hands on—so I sound really smart when we have conversations."

"That list should keep you busy," Lexi said.

"True. And I'll add more resolutions as I go along," Binky said. "This is just a start. I'll tell you about them when I decide what's next."

"I'm sure we're going to be hearing all about it." Binky might be the one wanting self-improvement, but none of the girls had any doubt that they'd all get sucked into her enthusiasm.

"I think your plan sounds great, Binky. I hope it works out very well." Lexi gave a cat-like stretch. "As for me, I'm starved. Mom said she was going to bake chocolate chip cookies this morning. Anybody want one?"

"Your mom makes the world's best cookies," Jennifer said. "I'll never say no."

"They're better than the ones at that cookie store in the mall," Peggy added. "Do you think she made them with macadamia nuts this time?"

A little whimper came from Binky's corner of the room. "Chocolate chip macadamia nut cookies?" She looked as though she were about to drool all over her shoes. "I *love* chocolate chip macadamia nut cookies."

"Then come downstairs and have one," Lexi invited.

"Weren't you listening to me at all?" Binky

wailed. "What about my self-improvement program?"

"Binky, you're the size of a toothpick. One cookie won't hurt you."

"But I can't eat just one. You know that."

"Even four cookies won't hurt you. Come on."

"What about all the fat and the sugar?"

"Have a glass of juice while we eat," Lexi offered.

"Juice? No thanks. I'll start my self-improvement program tomorrow." A grin lit Binky's features. "That's what I'll do. I'll just start tomorrow. Come on. What are we waiting for? Let's go down and get those cookies!"

Cookies and milk in hand, the girls walked into Mrs. Leighton's cheerful studio. The room was an eclectic clutter of easels, tables, and canvases. Several paintings in various stages of completion hung on the walls. A portrait of Lexi and Ben was the focal point of the room. Mrs. Leighton, in jeans and a paint-spattered sweatshirt, was at her easel putting finishing touches on a delicate flower. Oddly, she was wearing sunglasses.

"Hello, girls. I see you found the cookies. I heard you come in after school, but I was so involved in this project I just didn't want to quit. How's it looking?"

"Great!" Jennifer said admiringly. "You're the best artist I know."

Binky concurred.

"That's very flattering. I need all the praise I can get right now. I'm a little nervous about my upcoming show."

"I hate to sound snoopy or anything, Mrs. Leighton," Binky ventured, "but why are you wearing sunglasses?"

"Oh, sorry," Mrs. Leighton slipped them off and tucked one bow into the waistband of her jeans. "How silly of me. It seemed awfully bright in here. It was easier for me to see with the glasses on, that's all."

"Mom, it's not unusually bright in here today. You're the one who likes this room because it's a northern exposure."

"It's very strange, isn't it?" Mrs. Leighton shrugged off the odd event nonchalantly. "My eyes have been bothering me lately. Perhaps I need glasses. Your father says I've been squinting a lot."

"I didn't realize you'd been having trouble with your eyes," Binky said.

"Not 'trouble,' really. It's just that when I start to paint on a white canvas, I'm bothered by the glare. It gives me a headache. I've always enjoyed the windows in this room, but lately I've wished that I'd put shades on them so I could darken it a bit."

"My mom always gets headaches when she needs her glasses changed," Peggy said.

"I'm sure that's all it is," Mrs. Leighton said lightly as her fingers drifted to her temple. "But I do have a terrible headache. Maybe I should take a break and have one of those cookies myself."

"Is that why you've been pulling the drapes in the living room lately?" Lexi wondered, refusing to be diverted. "The house is always dark when I come home from school."

"Sunshine and light fade carpets and upholsteries, you know," Mrs. Leighton said. "I really should have been protecting the furniture all along."

"You've never cared about that before," Lexi persisted.

"You've probably been working too hard, Mrs. Leighton." Peggy glanced around the room. "This place is *filled* with artwork."

"You're right. I've been driving myself crazy trying to get enough good work done for the show."

"Is it that important?"

"It's been one of my goals to be known as a talented local artist," Mrs. Leighton admitted. "This is my first big break. If I show well here, it will establish my reputation in the community. It certainly wouldn't hurt to sell more canvases."

"I think you should get some rest," Binky interjected. "Otherwise you might get sick and not be able to do your show anyway. That's what my mom would say."

"Your mother's a very wise woman." Mrs. Leighton smiled. "And I *do* plan to rest as soon as I get this canvas completed. And after that, I'm going to have my eyes checked." She picked up her brush again and stared at the canvas. "I think a touch of umber right here would be a good idea, don't you?" Her voice trailed away as she lost herself in her work. The girls left the studio quietly.

When they reached the kitchen, Jennifer turned to Lexi. "Do you think it's weird that your mom's wearing sunglasses to paint?"

"Mom's been under a lot of strain lately," Lexi admitted. "She hasn't been herself. Dad's commented on it too. We both think she'll be better once the show is over. Then mom can get back to normal."

"What do you mean, 'normal'?" Jennifer wondered.

"Oh, nothing big. Just a lot of little things. Sometimes she complains about seeing spots before her eyes. She gets upset easily too. Once, when she'd been working all day and most of the night, she had this weird spell and couldn't see at all."

"That's scary." Binky looked alarmed.

"I know. I thought so too, but mom brushed it off like it was nothing. She's not letting anything get in the way of this art show."

"Have other weird things been happening?" Peggy appeared concerned.

"Not really. Sometimes when I come into the studio, Mom's shaking her hands—like this." Lexi demonstrated, flapping her hands limply in front of her. "She says they feel weak. I suppose that's from holding her arm at such an uncomfortable angle to paint. Sometimes her hands tremble."

"Does she have trouble walking too?" Jennifer wondered.

"Sometimes when she's really tired, I've noticed that she drags one leg. I mentioned it to her and she laughed it off. She said she was too lazy to lift it."

"She definitely needs more rest," Peggy concluded. "She's going to make herself sick if she keeps working this hard."

"I agree with you," Lexi said somberly, "but I don't know what to do. Mom's stubborn and independent. If she wants to work, it's pretty hard to stop her."

"I wonder if your mother would like join my self-improvement program?" Binky said. "Maybe she and I could work together on projects. It sounds as though she needs it as much as I do!"

# Chapter Two

"Lexi, will you set the table for supper?" Mrs. Leighton stood at the stove frying steaks. "Benjamin, you'll have to move those papers."

"Aw," Lexi's little brother protested, but he gathered together his pictures and crayons.

Lexi closed her math book. "I'm glad supper's almost ready. I'm starved."

As Lexi went to the cupboard, Ben cleared the table. Wiggles, Ben's half-grown puppy, snorted and snuffled in his sleep. He'd been napping on Ben's shoes and had protested when Ben stood up.

"Who was the last one to use the garbage disposal?" Dr. Leighton asked. He bent over the sink and peered into the dark recesses with a small flashlight. "It looks like somebody tried to grind up a spoon in here."

"Not me," Ben chimed.

"Or me," Lexi said promptly.

"Or me," Mrs. Leighton added. "That leaves you and Wiggles as the possible guilty party."

"Very funny." Dr. Leighton plunged his hand into the sink and pulled out a battered kitchen teaspoon.

"Marilyn, is this from your good silverware?"

Mrs. Leighton turned around to answer. "S . . . spool gool froshslep. . . ." Even she was startled by the words that came out of her mouth.

"What did you say?" Dr. Leighton looked confused.

"Fragool shlep. . . ." Mrs. Leighton tried to speak, but the mumbled words came out in the same strange mishmash.

"What?"

Lexi and Ben moved toward their mother as Mrs. Leighton clung to the edge of the counter, her eyes wide and alarmed. Slowly she found the words, "I said, 'the spoon is from my good set.' "

"That's not what it sounded like the first time," Ben said.

Dr. Leighton moved quickly toward his wife and took her arm. "What's wrong?"

"I don't know. The words turned to mush in my mouth. What I was thinking and what I was saying were two entirely different things." Mrs. Leighton looked genuinely puzzled. "I've never had something like that happen to me before."

"It was weird, Mom," Ben observed. "We couldn't understand you!"

"You sounded like a tape player with the batteries wearing out. Your voice got slower and slower and the words came out all slurred."

"I know, honey, I couldn't even understand myself." Mrs. Leighton passed her hands across her eyes. "I guess I had my brain in gear before my mouth."

Dr. Leighton didn't like her explanation. "I think you'd better sit down."

"I just mumbled a little, that's all. I don't know

why it happened, but I'm sure it won't happen again."

"I think Dad's right," Lexi said. "I'll finish cooking the steaks."

"I'm tired. Getting ready for this show has worn me out. . . ." Suddenly Mrs. Leighton pitched forward and caught herself on the counter. A glass sitting on the edge clattered to floor and smashed.

Dr. Leighton helped her to a kitchen chair. She sat heavily, a dazed expression on her face.

"What's wrong, Mom? What happened?" Ben's brown almond-shaped eyes were large and frightened. Ben, as a Down's syndrome child, was extremely sensitive to weakness or suffering in others.

Mrs. Leighton sat quietly. Her skin was pale and her eyes were glazed. She lifted a trembling hand to her forehead and scraped away a strand of hair. "I just had the oddest sensation," she finally murmured.

"What do you mean?" Lexi set a glass of water in front of her mother. Mrs. Leighton's hand trembled as she took it.

"I can't explain it. Nothing painful. Just these odd feelings."

"You're going to have to be a little clearer than that." Dr. Leighton sounded stern, a sure sign he was frightened.

"My legs felt heavy."

Ben stared at his mother's legs. "They don't *look* fat."

Mrs. Leighton smiled weakly. "Not 'fat,' Ben. *Heavy,* like they were made of stone and I couldn't lift them. For a moment, I felt very weak. Maybe

I've been standing at my easel too much lately."

"This has happened before?" Dr. Leighton asked sharply.

"Once or twice. Always when I've been working hard to finish a painting. Sometimes when I back up to take a good look at my canvas my leg drags. Isn't it strange?"

Dr. Leighton's eyebrows knit together in a scowl. "Why haven't you told me about this before now?"

"Because I never thought about it again after it happened. With a little rest the weakness and limp went away. I know I've been working too hard. The show will be over soon and then I'm going to take an entire week to do nothing but rest."

"Have you had any *other* symptoms you haven't told me about?" Lexi's father wondered.

"Well, I *have* been stiff a lot, especially when I've perched too long on a stool in front of my easel. My leg stiffens and I can't bend it at the knee. It loosens up after awhile, though. Just like my vision clears up after a bit."

"Vision?" Dr. Leighton said sharply.

Lexi explained to her father what had happened to her mother in the studio that afternoon.

Mrs. Leighton waved her hand in the air to dismiss what her daughter was saying. "Don't take this so seriously! What's a numb hand or toe? A little clumsiness or fatigue? Nothing—not after the way I've been working!"

Mrs. Leighton ran her fingers through her hair and attempted to smile. "I'll be as relieved as you will be when this art show is over." She sighed. "I never dreamed it would be this hard on me. Maybe I'm not cut out to be a professional artist. Perhaps

I can't take the pressure."

"Why don't you lie down for a while, Mom?"

"I think that's an excellent idea. Come on," Dr. Leighton said. "I'll help you upstairs to bed."

"I don't want to go to bed."

"You may not *want* to, but that's where you're going. Lexi will bring up a tray with your supper. In fact, I'll eat upstairs with you. How does that sound?"

"Rather romantic," Mrs. Leighton teased, trying to break the somber mood in the kitchen.

"Good. Glad to hear it." Dr. Leighton bent down, scooped his wife into his arms, and carried her toward the stairs. Lexi heard them laughing as they reached the top of the staircase.

After she'd finished the steaks and dished up the potatoes and vegetables, she carried two trays upstairs. Her mother was in bed, resting against a nest of pillows. There was more color in her cheeks and she looked positively cheerful.

"I'm sorry, darling. I ruined supper for everyone tonight."

"No you didn't, Mom. You're just tired. Rest is good for you. Ben and I can manage alone downstairs," Lexi assured her parents. "Don't worry a bit about us. We'll be fine."

Twenty minutes later, Lexi wasn't so sure it would be fine after all. Ben was frightened, pouty, and more than a little angry that his parents had deserted him at dinnertime.

"I want my mom and dad." He thrust his lower lip out and stared at the food on his plate.

"Ben, Mom's not feeling well. Dad's eating upstairs with her. What's wrong with having supper with me?"

"I want my mom and dad." His lower lip began to wobble. "Is Mom going to die?" Two big tears formed on his lower lashes.

Lexi walked around the table to hug her little brother. "Oh, Ben, of course not! She's just very tired. You've seen all the pictures she's painted. You know how hard she's worked in the last few weeks."

"I don't like it when my mom's sick," Ben said flatly.

Lexi had never seen Ben like this before. Of course, neither of them had ever seen their mother ill. Mrs. Leighton rarely even caught a cold. It was understandable that Ben was frightened.

"Eat your supper. We'll do the dishes together and then play a game. Your choice."

Ben perked up. "Dominoes?"

"You always win at dominoes!"

"Checkers?" A grin finally crossed Ben's features.

"Checkers? You're tougher to beat at checkers than you are at dominoes!"

"That's what I want to play. Checkers and dominoes."

Lexi, happy to see a smile return to her little brother's face, would have played checkers and dominoes all night just to keep it there. Finally, about ten o'clock, Ben began to yawn and rub his eyes.

After Lexi had tucked him into bed, listened to his prayers, and given him a good-night kiss, she walked down the hall to her parents' room.

Mrs. Leighton was asleep, one hand resting

gently against her cheek, her hair fanned across the pillow. Dr. Leighton sat next to the bed staring at her, his hands folded. Lexi slipped away without speaking. She knew her father was praying.

---

"Hi! Whatcha up to?" Binky walked into Lexi's kitchen without knocking. "Every teacher really piled on the homework today. Can you believe it? I finished most of mine during study hall."

Lexi was amazed. "*You* finished your work in study hall? I thought you always referred to study hall as 'social hour.' "

"That was before my self-improvement program! Now I'm maximizing my time. Did you know that if you actually *pay attention* in class, and then use the fifteen minutes at the end of the hour to work on your homework, you can get most of it done?"

"Really? What a discovery!" Lexi said sarcastically.

"I've been wasting my evenings doing homework in front of the television when I could have gotten it done in class! It sure took me a long time to figure that out."

"Binky, you're too much!"

Binky wasn't listening. She dug in the pocket of her jeans until she pulled out a ratty piece of paper.

"I've been feeling so good about myself since I've been on this self-improvement program that I think my friends should join me. It would be much easier, you know, if we had a little support group going."

"Support group?" Lexi asked suspiciously. This new Binky was almost harder to take than the old careless one. She closed her textbook and stared at her friend.

"Someone to talk to, someone to call in the middle of the night when you're just about to eat an entire pint of almond fudge ice cream and you know you shouldn't. Exercise partners. It's much easier to do these things in pairs, you know."

"What are you planning to do? *Assign* people to a self-improvement program?"

Binky's eyes brightened. "That's a great idea. I'm glad you thought of it. Even you could use a little self-improvement. Sometimes I think you're practically perfect, but in my heart I know you're not. I know how you love chocolate. You should cut that out. It's got way too much fat and sugar. And you and Todd eat too many banana splits. Todd should be watching his diet too. What's the point of weight lifting or doing exercises if he isn't taking care of his insides?" Binky made a note on her scrap of paper. "I'm going to tell him that the next time I see him."

Lexi stared open-mouthed at her friend.

"And Peggy! Do you know that she goes to school without breakfast? Have you considered how bad that is for you? She'd be much more alert during the day if she'd eat something—juice, a little cereal, a piece of toast . . ."

"Binky, you can't just order people to do these things."

"Why not? It's good for them. I'd be doing everyone a favor." Binky chewed on the end of her pen. "I can see where some problems might come up, though."

"Oh, really?" Lexi's tone was sarcastic, but Binky ignored it.

"Jennifer, for example. I don't even know where to *start* with *her*. She doesn't eat right; she doesn't exercise. She never reads a book. She hates to study. She's always overdrawing her checking account." Binky threw her hands in the air. "That girl needs a self-improvement counselor!"

"You aren't thinking . . ."

"Oh no. Not me." Binky shook her head. "I'm going to have my hands full with Egg."

"You're going to put your brother on a self-improvement program too?"

"Egg needs one most of all. Have you looked at that boy lately? He's skinnier than ever. He needs to eat right and to lift weights to bulk up a bit. When he stands sideways in a strong breeze, he practically blows over. And do you think Egg knows anything about world politics? Not one thing. He's totally uneducated when it comes to the planet. I'll be working full time on myself and Egg."

Binky rambled cheerfully about her plans for her friends. Lexi knew that everyone would listen politely to Binky's grandiose ideas and then ignore her. A problem would arise only if Binky was too persistent with this self-improvement kick of hers. Binky was sometimes very hard to ignore.

"Have you got anything to eat?" Binky wondered.

"There's cake left from supper last night."

"Something healthy. Rice cakes, or watercress. Maybe some lentil soup."

"I could probably find a carrot if you wanted one."

"That would be fine. Could I have a carrot and a piece of paper?"

While Binky was gnawing on the carrot, Lexi pulled out a notebook.

"What do you want this for?"

"I want to work out my self-improvement schedule. I need to plan my day so I can fit everything into it." Binky busied herself drawing a chart on the empty page. While she was doing so, the back door opened and Benjamin burst inside.

"Hi! We got groceries."

"So that's where you were." Lexi ruffled her little brother's hair. "I tied Wiggles outside. You'd better play with him for a while."

"Okay." Ben raced past his mother, who placed her groceries on the counter and moved across the room to the table. She was walking with a very odd gait, dragging one foot and staggering slightly from side to side.

"Mom, are you all right?" Lexi stared at her mother.

Mrs. Leighton stumbled. Catching herself on the edge of the table, she lowered herself into a kitchen chair. "My, that was silly of me," she said breathlessly.

Lexi stared at her mother in bewilderment. "What did you do, Mom?"

"I stumbled on something." She looked down at the floor. There was nothing there. "I guess I tripped over my own feet." Mrs. Leighton's words slurred slightly as she spoke.

"Mrs. Leighton, are you drunk?"

As Lexi and Mrs. Leighton stared at her, Binky clamped her hand over her mouth and blushed furiously. "I didn't mean to ask that. It just came out. I'm *so* sorry."

"Binky, how *could* you?"

Mrs. Leighton raised a hand to silence Lexi. "Don't scold her. It's an honest question. I *was* behaving strangely. It's the exhaustion. I'll be so thankful once this art show is over." She put a trembling hand to her forehead. "Will you girls help me put these groceries away?"

"I'll do it." Binky eagerly jumped to the task, ready to make amends for her thoughtless comment.

"Binky, you're too much," Lexi muttered. But she helped her friend empty the grocery sacks and by the time they were done, all three were laughing.

---

"There's your mom," Todd said as Mrs. Leighton pulled into the driveway near the school. "She's got Ben with her."

Lexi hoisted her schoolbag to her shoulder and walked toward her parents' car. Todd and Egg followed her.

"Hi, Mrs. Leighton. How are you doing?" Todd leaned toward the car, his golden blond hair ruffling in the wind.

"Hello, boys. It's good to see you."

"What's up?" Egg wondered.

"Benjamin and Lexi have appointments to get their teeth cleaned," Mrs. Leighton explained.

Ben pouted in the backseat, "My teeth *are* clean. I brushed and brushed and brushed."

"That doesn't matter, Ben. You still have to go to the dentist."

"But, Mom . . ." Ben hated going to the dentist. He was trying to be brave but it wasn't working very well.

"How is your brother Mike, Todd?" Mrs. Leighton asked. "I haven't seen him for a long time."

"He keeps busy. His garage business is really taking off. He's talking about hiring another mechanic."

Mrs. Leighton glanced at her watch. "It's time to go or we're going to be late."

Lexi and Ben waved at Todd and Egg as Mrs. Leighton pulled away. They hadn't gone very far when Mrs. Leighton made a clucking sound at the back of her throat. "I think I should take this car to Mike's garage right now. It's not working very well."

"What do you mean?" The car seemed to be fine, Lexi thought, but not her *mother*. Mrs. Leighton was having trouble moving her foot back and forth between the gas pedal and the brake.

"Mom, look out!"

Mrs. Leighton jerked the wheel sharply to the left. The car swerved, barely missing a vehicle in the oncoming lane. They ran off the road, down the slope of the ditch, and up again until they rested on a grassy incline. For a moment everyone was silent. Then Ben began to cry in terrified gulping sobs.

"Lexi, Benjamin, are you all right?" Mrs. Leighton sounded shocked and stunned.

"I think so. We had our seat belts on. What happened?"

"I don't know. My foot wouldn't move from the gas pedal to the brake. I pulled to the side and . . ."

Mrs. Leighton seemed to be in shock. "Now what have I done?"

"It's okay, Mom. I think I can back out. Let me try." Lexi didn't feel comfortable letting her mother drive again. She appeared very shaken.

Mrs. Leighton braced herself against the car as she moved around the vehicle into the passenger seat. Lexi slipped behind the wheel and backed slowly down the incline, up the ditch, and back onto the road. "Maybe we shouldn't go to the dentist today. Let's go home. We'll cancel and make the appointments for later."

They reached the house without incident. Dr. Leighton met them at the door.

"There you are! I've been waiting for . . . what's wrong?"

The story spilled out and Dr. Leighton listened intently. "Could it have been the brake on the car, Marilyn?" he finally asked. "Think, now. This is important. I realize that you're blaming yourself because you haven't been feeling well lately, but if those brakes are going bad . . ."

"I don't think so, Jim, but it happened so quickly, I couldn't say for sure."

"That settles it. Tomorrow I'm taking the car in for an overhaul."

"What about Mom?" Ben wondered. "Does she need an 'overhaul' too?"

The Leightons all burst out laughing. Dr. Leighton ruffled his son's hair. "Not quite like the car, Ben, but it might not hurt to have your mother go to the doctor for a check-up too. Then, when both Mom and the car get a clean bill of health, we can quit worrying."

Ben nodded cheerfully, seeming satisfied by his father's answer. It was some time later, however, when Lexi found Ben curled in a ball in the middle of the living room.

"What's wrong with my mom," he asked, his voice trembling.

"Nothing's wrong."

"Yes, there is."

Quietly Lexi put her arm around her little brother's shoulders and led him to the couch. They sat down and held each other. Finally, Lexi spoke, "I don't know what's wrong with Mom, Benjamin. I'm worried too."

# Chapter Three

Peggy Madison, Jennifer Golden, Anna Marie Arnold, Angela Hardy, and Lexi Leighton had all gathered at Binky McNaughton's house at Binky's request. No one was happy.

"Get on with it, Binky," Jennifer grumbled. "I haven't got all day. When you called us, you acted as if there were an emergency and now we're sitting here twiddling our thumbs."

Binky paced back and forth in front of them, her brow furrowed. "Just give me a minute to gather my thoughts."

"You'll need more than a minute for that, Binky. You're going to need a lifetime."

Peggy poked Jennifer in the side. "Shhh. Don't irritate her. She's building up to something."

Binky stopped pacing and faced her friends. "This is very difficult for me to say, but it has to be done—for your own good."

"Oh, oh," Angela mumbled. "When Egg or Binky say something is for our 'own good,' that means something bad is going to happen."

Angela dated Binky's older brother Egg. She knew what kind of turmoil the McNaughtons could cause with their good intentions. While Angela and her mother were homeless and living at the mission, Egg had spent a night on the street pretending to be homeless in an attmept to understand how it must feel. The McNaughtons would stop at nothing to get a point across.

"None of us are as fit or as firm as we should be."

"Speak for yourself," Jennifer protested. "I'm as firm as I want to be. Who's looking anyway?"

"We all have character flaws that could be improved," Binky continued, ignoring Jennifer. "Because we're such good friends, we've been overlooking all these little quirks and flaws that should be corrected."

"We haven't been overlooking yours, Binky. We keep telling you about them, but you never do anything to change."

Again, Binky ignored her friend. "I've decided," she continued, "that if *I'm* going to go on a self-improvement program, my friends should too."

"If you were drowning in the middle of the ocean, would you expect us to go down with you?" Anna Marie asked.

"It's not the same thing. Drowning isn't good for you. Self-improvement is. You'll all thank me when we're done."

"I'm done now." Jennifer stood up, ready to leave.

"Stay right where you are." Binky pointed a finger in Jennifer's direction. "Don't move a muscle. We have things to do."

Jennifer, surprised at the force behind Binky's tone, sat down. Smiling, Lexi covered her mouth with her hand. It wasn't often that someone got the best of Jennifer.

"I thought it would be nice of me to point out the things that *you* people need to work on. That would make your self-improvement plan much easier."

"*You* are going to tell us what's wrong with us and how to fix it?"

"Something like that. I'm going to give you some friendly, helpful tips that will make your life better in the long run." Binky picked up a stack of papers lying on a table. "First of all, I made a list of the things each of you should work on. I'll hand that out." She busied herself with the papers. The girls stared at one another in disbelief.

"Can you believe this is happening?" Angela whispered to Lexi.

"I knew it was coming but I just didn't know how to stop it," Lexi murmured helplessly.

"Each of you can go over your list and decide what steps you need to take. I put the suggestion to cut fat intake on each list. If you're drinking whole milk, switch to skim. If you're putting butter and jelly on your toast, skip the butter and just use jelly. Cut the obvious fat off your meat."

Binky picked up another stack of papers. "Here's a list of all our favorite foods and the number of fat grams in each. Read this over. You'll notice it's much smarter to eat a piece of angel food cake than it is to eat a piece of chocolate cake."

"Boring!" Jennifer interjected.

"Jennifer, you're my friend. I can't let you clog your arteries. You're just going to have to listen to me."

Binky pulled a tagboard graph from behind the couch.

"What's *that*?"

"Just a little demonstration to show you how *dangerous* eating the wrong foods can be."

"Don't kid us, Binky. What can a piece of chocolate cake do? It's not like it's going to stage a drive-by shooting or anything."

Binky glared at Jennifer. "What did you have for breakfast this morning?"

"A blueberry muffin and a glass of milk."

"Whole or skim milk?"

"Two percent. What's your point?"

Binky pointed dramatically at a line on her graph. "Blueberry muffins can have up to 34 grams of fat in them! And two-percent milk gets 36 percent of its calories from fat. Do you realize heart disease is the number one killer of men and women in this country? And do you realize that if you continue to eat this way, you could be one of those statistics?"

Jennifer appeared startled. "Hey! I thought I was eating a pretty *good* breakfast!"

"Our goal should be to get only 20 percent of our calories from fat. Now if you'll study the sheets I've given you . . ."

"It's all a bad dream," Peggy kept saying to herself. "She's not doing this to us."

"Wake up and kiss hot fudge brownie delights goodbye," Jennifer hissed.

Binky paced in front of them, her hands clasped behind her back, her head tipped forward as though she were studying the toes of her shoes as she walked. "This is very difficult for me," she said, "because you are my dearest friends in the whole world and I want the very best for you. It's hard to tell people where they're flawed."

"Flawed? What do you mean by that?"

"I'm talking to you girls first because I've been dreading telling my brother Egg what I have planned for him. If it's any comfort, Egg has *many* more flaws than any of you."

Angela and Lexi did all they could to keep from bursting into laughter.

"You all need to exercise more." Binky looked up to see the reaction to her statement. "Now is the time to start doing aerobic exercise to keep our cardiovascular systems healthy. And weight training is very important for the muscles."

Jennifer gave a huge snort. "Muscles? Binky, what are you talking about? Have you looked at the size of your arms lately? I have *pencils* fatter than your arms."

Binky looked injured and indignant. "I didn't say I'd been weight training *yet*. I said I'm going to start and that I think all of you should too. I checked with the athletic department at school. Anyone can use the weight room as long as the coaches aren't using it for training. I'm getting a schedule from the athletic director's office tomorrow so we'll all know when we can use the machines."

"I don't like the way she says 'we,' " Anna Marie muttered.

"Anna Marie, I'm glad you spoke up. Very good."

Anna Marie looked startled at Binky's odd response.

"We all know that you are shy."

Anna Marie blushed.

"That's why you should plan to meet one new

person every week. *I* meet lots of people in the cafeteria."

"Binky, you usually meet them because you dump food on their heads or spill milk at their feet. No one is ever very happy to meet *you* in the cafeteria."

"I'm a little klutzy, that's all. Anna Marie doesn't have to spill anything. She can just walk over to someone, sit down, say hi, and have lunch with them. That's all."

"What if I want to eat lunch with my friends?" Anna Marie asked, dazed by Binky's scheme.

"Do this one day a week and you'll get over your shyness in a hurry. It's a great self-improvement tip. What do you say?"

"I'll think about it," Anna Marie said noncommittally.

Jennifer stood up. "Binky, you've gone too far this time."

"I'm glad you said that, Jennifer, because you're next on my list. Did you read the handout I gave you?"

"No."

"That's my point! You never read *anything*. I realize that you're dyslexic and it's hard for you to read, but you shouldn't completely avoid the written word. Listen to books on tape instead."

"Actually, that sounds like a pretty good idea," Lexi murmured.

"You're creating a monster." Jennifer turned to Lexi. "Now she's encouraged!"

"Let's make a promise to one another," Binky continued, ignoring the disgruntled chatter around her. *"No more sodas."*

"Are you kidding?" Peggy gasped.

"Caffeine sucks the calcium right out of your bones. From now on, we're all going to drink water when we're thirsty, right?"

"Speak for yourself," Peggy said.

"Pick on somebody else," Jennifer growled.

"Angela has to quit chewing her nails," Binky said bluntly. "And Lexi really should start saving money. Lexi, every time we're together, you're buying fabric for a sewing project. You're too busy to get it all done. You should start putting your money in a savings account instead."

"Binky, you're the girl who can't keep a penny in her pocket longer than five minutes!"

"I gave myself the same self-improvement rule. If we have to be financially responsible together, it will be easier."

"So far, we haven't heard much about what *you're* doing, Binky," Anna Marie said slyly. "When are you going to tell us about *that*?"

"Yeah, how are you going to 'improve' yourself?" Jennifer asked. "Since you've got all these great plans for us, you *must* have many more for yourself."

"Of course I have a plan for myself! I'm going to start flossing my teeth every day."

Peggy and Jennifer hooted with laughter. "*That's* your big self-improvement plan? We're supposed to pump iron and give up the foods we love so you can floss your teeth?"

"And I'm not going to skip breakfast anymore, either. That's very bad for a person."

"This isn't fair. If you're going to tell us what *we*

have to do to improve, then we should be able to tell *you* what you need to do."

"But *I'm* the one who came up with the self-improvement idea!"

"And if you want us to be involved in it, you'll have to let us tell you what we think you need to do."

Binky's zeal for changing the lives of her friends appeared tarnished by the thought that her friends had plans for her too. "It's very nice of you to offer, but I think I have everything pretty well under control right now. A little exercise, a few less fat grams, and . . ."

"You told me you wanted to be as spectacular as the girls at Harry's college," Lexi said. "We can help you do that, if you'll listen to us."

"That might have been the motivating factor in the beginning. . . ."

Peggy lifted a strand of Binky's hair and rolled it between her fingers. "You're definitely going to have to change your hair," she said.

Jennifer nodded. "A new cut. Binky, most of the time your hair looks like you stuck your head in a pencil sharpener and had someone turn the handle. It's time for you to get a professional job."

Binky's hands went to her head. "You don't like my hair?"

"And you have to learn how to put on some makeup," Angela added. "You're a very cute girl but sometimes those freckles are just too much."

One of Binky's hands slipped to the bridge of her nose.

"I agree with you about eating right and exercising," Lexi said. "That's good for all of us. It's just that you tend to get a little bossy sometimes."

"But we can be bossy right back," Peggy assured her. "And ultimately you'll love us for it. Especially when Harry sees how you've changed."

"I don't know." Binky sounded worried. "Harry says he likes me just the way I am."

"All you need," Jennifer said as she circled Binky, eyeing her jeans and faded sweatshirt, "is a new look and new clothes. Something that shows off your tiny figure instead of covering it up."

"I *like* my clothes. They're comfortable."

"Self-improvement can't always be comfortable," Anna Marie pointed out.

The girls were dissecting Binky's taste in clothing when Egg McNaughton wandered into the room carrying a huge bowl of popcorn dripping with melted butter. The warm fragrance was tantalizing. "What's everybody doing here?" Egg asked through a mouthful. There was a dab of butter on the tip of his chin.

"Binky called a meeting," Angela said.

"And you came? Are you nuts?" As Egg walked by his sister, Binky's hand snaked out. She dug deep into the bowl of popcorn.

Jennifer clamped a firm hand around Binky's wrist. "Drop it."

"What?" Binky looked at Jennifer with round eyes.

"Drop the popcorn."

Binky's fingers opened and the popcorn fell back into the bowl, leaving her hand coated with butter. "Why? Popcorn is healthy."

"Not with all that butter on it," Peggy said. "Look at your hand. It's full of grease. That could be coating your arteries right now."

"But I'm hungry," Binky protested.

"Then make some popcorn in the air popper," Lexi suggested.

"Without butter, it tastes like cardboard," Binky protested.

"Too bad. You have to practice what you preach. If you want us to be on your self-improvement kick, you'd better be the leader."

Binky stared longingly at Egg's bowl. "I hate popcorn without butter and salt."

"But you can learn to live without it." Angela took Binky by the elbow and steered her toward the kitchen.

"And leave you alone in here with Egg and that bowl? Are you kidding?" Binky turned around and put her fists on her hips. She looked like a little wet hen. "You're trying to trick me. You want me out of here so you can help Egg eat that popcorn. Well, I'm not leaving."

"Then I guess we'd better," Jennifer said with a wide smile. "We have lots to think about now that you've given us your suggestions for personal self-improvement."

Egg, who had been listening to all of this with a confused expression on his face, shook his head and dug into the popcorn.

"And, Egg, no matter what your sister says or does or how hard she pleads, *do not* let her have any of your popcorn."

Egg grinned. "Gladly."

"And if you see her go into the kitchen and make some of her own and put butter on it, stop her immediately. Binky is giving up fat in her diet and she needs all the help she can get."

"That's terrific. Make Egg part of the fat police. I'll never get to eat another thing," Binky groused.

"How does it feel to be told what to do, Binky?" Peggy asked.

"It feels icky. I don't like it very much. . . ." A dawning expression flickered on Binky's features. "Oh, I see what you mean."

"We're glad you're worried about us, Binky. We just don't like your tactics."

Binky was subdued as Angela and Peggy said goodbye at the front door.

Lexi and Jennifer remained until Egg had polished off the last of his popcorn. Then they said goodbye, leaving Binky—pouting—in the hands of her brother.

---

"What are we going to do about Binky?" Jennifer wondered as she and Lexi walked toward the Leightons' house. "That girl is going to drive us all nuts."

"Humor her. Binky's intentions are good. She wants to improve and she thinks that it would be good for us to improve too."

"Binky is going to forget all about her own self-improvement plan as soon as she gets *us* going on her little project. You saw how she acted when Egg walked into the room carrying that popcorn!"

Both girls were laughing when they entered the back door of the Leighton house. Mrs. Leighton was seated at the kitchen counter, her hands folded in front of her, her eyes cast down. She looked as though she'd been crying. The laughter died on Lexi's lips.

"Mom, what's wrong?"

There were several canned goods and a broken grocery bag on the floor behind Mrs. Leighton. A checkbook and a stack of bills lay before her on the counter. When Mrs. Leighton looked up, her eyes were brimming with anguish.

"I don't know, Lexi. I've never been so frustrated in my entire life."

"Why?"

"I feel so awkward and so clumsy. I've never been a klutz, but lately it seems I can't do anything right." Mrs. Leighton gestured toward the broken bag and cans on the floor. "I can't even put my groceries away without dropping things all over the place. I meant to put a bag of groceries on the counter but missed it entirely. They fell all over the floor. Why on earth would I do a thing like that?"

"Because you weren't paying attention?" Jennifer suggested timidly.

"But I *was* paying attention! That's what's so odd. The strangest things have been happening to me lately. The other night at supper, I reached out to pick up a glass of milk and I knocked it over. I stumble around as though my feet are too big for my body, knocking over plants and figurines that I've *never* bumped into in all the years I've owned them. Sometimes I think it's my vision that's deteriorating and sometimes I think it's my entire brain."

"We've been through this before, Mom. It's the art show. You're exhausted, that's all."

"If that's what's causing this, then I'll never do another art show."

"Don't say that, Mom."

"It's true. I've become a constant complainer. I

have stupid little aches and pains that seem to move around my body. My neck gets stiff and my leg feels like it's falling asleep. I feel exhausted all the time. You don't want to hear that from me anymore, Lexi, and I don't want to say it. There's nothing more boring than being tired all the time." Mrs. Leighton ran her fingers through her hair in frustration. "Maybe I'm just lazy."

"You're the least lazy person in the entire world!" Lexi said adamantly. "And you know that's true."

"Is it? I'm not sure anymore." A fresh wash of tears clouded Mrs. Leighton's eyes. "Even *Ben* scolded me today."

"That little stinker! What did he say?"

"Oh, don't blame him. He was telling the truth. When I picked him up from school, I wasn't feeling very well. My leg didn't want to stay on the gas pedal. I was very short with him. He started to cry and told me that I was in a bad mood all the time."

"He doesn't understand the pressure you're under."

"That doesn't give me any excuse to be irritable or temperamental. Besides, he's right. I *am* in a bad mood!"

Mrs. Leighton waved her hands over the papers in front of her. "I finally decided that if I couldn't do anything but spill things, I might as well sit down and pay some bills. At least that way I wouldn't break anything, but even that's not working. Now I'm having trouble writing out the checks."

"What do you mean?"

"Double vision. And my hand isn't cooperating either."

"Mom, have you considered making an appointment to see the doctor? Maybe you're not tired. Maybe you've got a virus or something."

"I've already called the clinic for an appointment. I'm going in tomorrow."

Quickly, Lexi crossed the kitchen and threw her arms around her mother's shoulders. "Everything's going to be fine, Mom. Wait and see. You're going to be all right."

Lexi wanted to believe her own words, but she wasn't sure she could.

# Chapter Four

Lexi could barely sit still. If class didn't end soon, she was going to explode. No matter how hard she tried, she couldn't tune in to her teacher's droning voice. All she could think about was her mother and what she might have learned at the clinic.

After what seemed like centuries, the class bell rang. Lexi bolted out of her desk and grabbed her books.

Todd caught up to her in the hallway. "What's with you? I thought you were going to eject right out of that chair in class."

"Have you got a minute?" Lexi asked.

"Actually, I do. I have a pass to go down to the *Cedar River Review* room."

They walked together down the hallway toward the newspaper staff room.

"I wanted to call you last night but I didn't feel comfortable spending time away from my mom."

"What's wrong? Is she sick?"

"I don't know. That's what's so scary." The story about her mother's behavior spilled from Lexi. She told of the weakness in Mrs. Leighton's hands and legs, the dizziness, the vision problems, fatigue, the strange gait she sometimes had when she walked, the clumsiness, and all the other odd symptoms that had popped up in recent weeks.

Todd looked genuinely alarmed. "That doesn't sound like your mother at all."

"I know. That's what's so frightening. I can hardly remember my mother having a cold or the flu. Now even her balance is messed up. I saw her holding on to the counter just to walk from the refrigerator to the sink."

"Trouble walking? Numbness in her hands? Trouble with her eyes? Dizziness? Fatigue? What kind of virus could that be?"

"I don't know. All these questions keep running through my mind. I need to know what's wrong with my mother."

"She's probably not home from the clinic yet," Todd pointed out logically. "So you may as well be in school. If you were home, you'd be pacing the floor, chewing your fingernails, and worrying even more. At least here there are people to distract you—like me."

He reached out and took her hand. There was little more he could say.

---

"Want to go to the Hamburger Shack with us after school? Peggy's already said she can come," Binky asked when she met Lexi by her locker.

Lexi arched one eyebrow. "I thought you were giving up the Hamburger Shack."

"I never said that. I said I was giving up fatty fried foods. I'm going to have a lettuce salad and a bagel." Binky's expression softened. "And I think you should come. You've looked so sad and worried all day that you've been scaring me. Come with us. We'll cheer you up."

"I can't. Thanks anyway, Bink. I need to go home. Mom should be home from her clinic appointment by now. I want to talk to her. I've had a horrible day worrying. Going to the Hamburger Shack will only prolong that."

"We'll miss you."

"Thanks, Bink." Lexi gave her friend a hug. "Even though you're driving us all crazy with this self-improvement thing, you're still a good friend. I appreciate it."

Binky bobbed her head. "I'll be thinking about you, Lexi."

---

Lexi made it from the school to her house in record time. Mrs. Leighton was in the kitchen washing paint out of some of her brushes.

"Mom?" Lexi's unspoken question hung in the air.

"Hello, honey. I stopped at the bakery and got some of your favorite rolls. Want one?"

"Not until I hear how you're doing. What did the doctor have to say?"

Mrs. Leighton shrugged. She looked fine, healthy. Better than Lexi remembered seeing her in days.

"He couldn't give me any conclusive answers. Crazy, isn't it? You can feel awful for days and then finally, when you get to a doctor, your symptoms seem to fly out the window. I felt like a hypochondriac making up complaints."

"We know you aren't making them up, Mom."

"The doctor realized that too. He ran some tests. We should have the results soon. Perhaps that will give us some clue as to what's going on with me."

"What kind of tests did he run?" Lexi wondered.

"All the usual—chest x-ray, blood tests. He also did an MRI."

"What's an MRI?"

"It's a different kind of x-ray called a 'magnetic resonance imager.' As the doctor explained it, it's not really an x-ray, because it doesn't involve any sort of radiation. The doctor says it's like being placed in a magnetic field and having radio wave pulses bounced off my body."

"Does it hurt?"

"Not at all. While the radio waves bounced off the magnetic field around me, a computer evaluated the results. It's very safe. No harmful x-rays or dyes needed to be injected into my body. The doctor says it's effective as well as accurate. The only part I didn't like was lying inside this tube-like machine for nearly an hour. I think I fell asleep. I must be even more tired than I realize."

"What is he looking for?" Lexi persisted.

"He didn't say. He said that there was no use discussing a possible diagnosis until all the tests were conducted. I agree with him. With an imagination as active as mine, I could scare myself worrying about possibilities that will never come to be.

"I don't want you to worry about this anymore either, Lexi. I've been to a very good doctor who's taken all the right tests. We'll wait for the results. Then we'll figure out what to do next. Most likely the doctor will say that I shouldn't plan any more art shows or subject myself to the stress involved with them."

Lexi nodded obediently and excused herself. Mom was right, she told herself. There was no use worrying now. They'd find out soon what the doctor had to say and then they'd deal with it. It probably was stress. The art show had been very hard on Mom. . . .

*Liar!* She was lying to herself and she knew it. No matter how many times she told herself that the art show was the cause of all this trouble, Lexi couldn't believe it. Mom was *sick*. And the thought of that made Lexi's insides curl and tighten until she felt like throwing up. Moms weren't supposed to be sick—ever. Kids got sick, not Moms. A mother was supposed to be strong. This twist of events had turned everything upside down for Lexi.

No matter how much Lexi or Ben coughed in Mom's face or curled next to her when they were ill, Mrs. Leighton never seemed to mind or suffer ill effects. Now, out of the blue, something had gone wrong.

Lexi spent the rest of the evening vainly attempting to assure herself that everything would be all right.

---

Much to Lexi's surprise, she'd become grateful for Binky's self-improvement program. Binky's nonsense kept Lexi from thinking too much about her mother. In fact, Binky seemed dead set on driving everyone crazy with this self-improvement thing.

"Are you coming to lunch with me?" Binky asked.

"I don't know," Lexi hesitated.

"Aren't you hungry?"

"Well, yes, but—"

"Then what's wrong?"

"Binky, I'm *embarrassed* to go to lunch with you. You've been policing everything that I or our friends eat. I watched you dig through Jerry's tray yesterday, making him exchange chocolate milk for skim."

"He thanked me for that," Binky said defensively. "Do you know how many fat grams are in chocolate milk?" She hoisted her book bag to her shoulder. One of the flaps fell open, revealing the corner of a red foil bag. Lexi reached out and snagged the item before Binky could cover it again.

"What's this?"

"Nothing. Stay out of my book bag, Lexi. That's not like you. You usually aren't snoopy."

"Cookies, Binky? Is this what you have in your bag? Cookies?"

"What's gotten into you? You've never searched my book bag before."

"And you've never had cookies in there when I couldn't have any," Lexi pointed out.

The red foil bag still contained three or four chocolate chip cookies. Lexi sniffed the bag. "These smell awfully fresh, Binky. I think you just opened them today."

"Give me my cookies."

Lexi held them away from Binky's grasp. "I don't think so. Not until you explain how they got in your book bag."

"What's this?" Jennifer Golden came up behind them. She took the cookie pouch out of Lexi's hand. "And where did you get this, Miss Leighton?"

"I got it out of Miss McNaughton's book bag."

Jennifer gave a theatrical gasp. "I can hardly believe it! Surely, Miss McNaughton would not have a *cookie* in her book bag. We all know how *bad* cookies are for a person."

"Quit it. Give me that bag." Binky grasped futilely for the bag, but Jennifer held it out of her reach.

"Binky, you're a hypocrite. You're telling everyone else what they should do, what they should eat, and how they should exercise. Then *you* go around sneaking cookies."

Binky's face crumbled. "I couldn't help it. I was starving. Egg watched me eat breakfast this morning, so all I dared have was an egg-white omelet and a piece of dry toast. It was terrible. I was so hungry that by the time I passed the convenience store on the way to school, I had to stop in and get something to eat.

"I went in to get a bottle of juice. I really did, but those cookies were sitting on the counter."

"And you heard them call your name?"

Binky hung her head. "Something like that."

"Here's the deal, Binky," Jennifer said. "You either do what you're making us do or you let us eat cookies too. Got it?"

Binky nodded.

"And if you don't ease up on all of us, I'm going to sit on you and force-feed you rice cakes and mineral water. Got that?"

Binky nodded again. "I don't know what the big

deal is all about," she muttered. "It's just a few cookies."

Jennifer handed her the bag. "Stuff your face. But remember not to be so hard on us next time we're eyeing a chocolate malt, all right?"

"Picky, picky," Binky muttered to herself. "Everyone is so picky. I try to do a good deed and what do I get? Trouble. Nothing but trouble." She walked away.

Jennifer and Lexi burst into laughter. "I love that girl," Jennifer said. "But if she doesn't quit telling us what to eat and when to exercise and how to wear our hair, there's going to be trouble. Even Minda Hannaford asked me today if I was on Binky's diet program."

Just then, Egg sauntered up to the two girls. "What's going on?"

"We just caught your sister with some contraband cookies." Lexi chuckled. "She had them hidden in her book bag. A secret snack."

"Doesn't surprise me a bit." Egg reached into his pocket and pulled out a candy bar. "If you opened the bottom drawer in my sister's dresser, you'd find it stashed with licorice. She *talks* about being a health nut, but deep in her heart, she's a junk food junkie. Now you know what I've been going through all my life. It's not easy living with Binky."

As he spoke, Egg polished off the candy bar, crumpled the wrapper and threw it into the garbage. Then he reached into another pocket and pulled out a second candy bar.

"You don't seem to be suffering too much from Binky's self-improvement program," Jennifer commented.

Egg grinned a chocolaty smile. "One thing I've learned from living with Binky is how to tune her out. When she starts telling me what to eat, I just don't listen. I have to keep this body of mine in fighting shape." With that, Egg ambled off down the hallway, his stick-like arms swinging at his sides and his scrawny, too-long-for-his-body legs leading him away from the girls.

Jennifer, Peggy and Lexi laughed until their laughter turned into hysterical tears. "*That's* the body Egg has to maintain with chocolate?" Jennifer gasped when she could finally speak again. "Poor Egg looks like a scarecrow!"

It wasn't until later that Lexi realized how grateful she was to Egg and Binky for provoking her laughter. They had allowed her to forget, for at least a few moments, her concerns about her mother.

---

"Have you heard from the doctor yet?" Lexi asked when she got home. Her mother was busy in the kitchen.

"Not yet."

"I thought you said you'd get the results soon."

"He said he'd call me, Lexi. That's all I can do. Besides, I don't have time to worry about the doctor right now. I'm feeling wonderfully well. I'm sure all my problems have been stress. The paintings are done and they're hung. Your dad took the afternoon off to help me at the gallery. Tonight is the show's opening. I'll be the guest of honor and you'll be my guest. It's going to be wonderful."

Lexi loved the way her mother looked. Her eyes

were shining and her step was brisk. Mrs. Leighton didn't look much older than a teenager herself. Lexi breathed an inward sigh of relief. Maybe it *was* stress that had caused all the problems in this house lately. Now that the time for the show opening was really here, perhaps things could get back to normal.

"Is it going to be boring?" Lexi wondered.

"Not at all. How could you be bored when your mother is the celebrated guest of honor?" Mrs. Leighton tweaked her daughter's cheek. "Wear that new black dress you made. I put some jewelry on your bed that I thought would look attractive with it. Ben's going to wear his suit and your father has rented a tux. The Leightons are going to be on display tonight and we want to look our best."

---

The gallery was spectacular. Pale hardwood floors gleamed beneath their feet. Long halls and arches dramatically highlighted Mrs. Leighton's paintings. What had looked good to Lexi at home looked absolutely spectacular here. There was a harpist playing music and a buffet table filled with hors d'oeuvres. Lexi was amazed at the number of people who had come out for this event.

A large woman came bearing down on her like a freight train. "And are you the daughter?"

"I guess so," Lexi said with a smile.

"Your mother is a very talented artist," the woman announced. "Her style is fresh and new. Do you paint?"

"No, not really."

"A pity," the large woman shook her head.

"Please extend my congratulations to your mother." She handed Lexi a business card. "I can't stay and your mother is surrounded by people right now, but I wanted her to know that I would be interested in hanging some of her work in my design studio. I'll get back to her next week."

"Yes, thank you. Thank you very much," Lexi stammered. The importance of this evening was finally beginning to dawn on her. The family had always thought Mrs. Leighton's talent was exceptional, but they hadn't realized *quite* how exceptional. Tonight, with all these people milling about, praising Mrs. Leighton's work, Lexi realized that her mother had the potential to become very well known.

It was after 11 o'clock when the last of the guests had departed and the Leightons were alone with the gallery director.

"Thank you for a wonderful evening," Mrs. Leighton said. "I never dreamed . . ."

The director smiled. "You're much too modest about your work. It has a great deal of appeal. I'm hoping for another show from you next year. Is that possible?"

"I don't know." Mrs. Leighton hesitated.

"We're scheduling eighteen months in advance. Why don't you look at your calendar and pick a date so I can put your name in our mailing? Several of your paintings sold tonight and I know more will go by the end of the month."

Lexi handed her mother the card she'd collected. "This lady said she'd like to hang some of your things in her design studio, Mom."

Mrs. Leighton's eyes widened. She handed the

card to the director. A big grin slid across his face. "There, you see! You're already into the exclusive design studio in Cedar River. You *have* to do another show for me next year."

"But it takes so much time and energy."

"Start now," the director said matter-of-factly. "It's what you *must* do if you want to make a name for yourself in the artistic community."

Mrs. Leighton glanced around the gallery—at the lights, the gleaming floors, the fountain bubbling in the center and all her beautiful pictures.

"I do want to *do* it," she said finally. "It's a dream come true for me. While Lexi and Ben were growing up, I painted with them, telling myself that someday, when they were older, I'd paint for myself. Now that I finally have the opportunity, I shouldn't pass it up."

"Absolutely right." The gallery director pumped Mrs. Leighton's hand enthusiastically. "Pop in one day this week and we'll discuss the details. I want you on our calendar. Thank you for a wonderful show."

---

"Ta dah!" Dr. Leighton opened the kitchen door with a flourish and gave a grand bow as he escorted his wife into the kitchen. Benjamin, giddy with excitement, ran to the counter. "Look what we made for you, Mom." He pulled the dish towel aside to reveal a layer cake decorated with chocolate frosting and multi-colored sprinkles.

"Lexi cooked it and I decorated," he said proudly. "It's your celebration cake."

"Why, Benjamin, it's absolutely beautiful. I'm

starved! I was so nervous at the opening that I didn't take a bite of food. Why don't you get the glasses, and I'll get the milk to have with our cake."

Suddenly, Mrs. Leighton gasped and fell heavily against the kitchen counter.

"Mom, what is it?"

"My leg, my leg. I can't move it. I can't move my leg." The color drained from Mrs. Leighton's face. Lexi's father was there in an instant. With one swift motion, he picked up his wife and carried her toward the couch. The party atmosphere evaporated, and the cake, cut but uneaten, was completely forgotten.

# Chapter Five

"Todd, Lexi, wait up!" Binky called to them from the doorway of the school. Her jacket was open and she was dragging her book bag on the ground. By the time she reached them, she was breathless.

"Do you want to hear the good news?" Her eyes were shining and there were high spots of color in her cheeks.

"You won a million dollars."

"Better! Better than a million dollars," Binky enthused.

"This *must* be good."

"Okay, Binky. What's your good news?"

"I've been working out in the weight room," Binky said in a confidential voice, "and I can bench press 40 pounds."

Todd and Lexi both stared at her blankly.

"Don't you see? My self-improvement plan is working! I couldn't bench press *anything* before I started and now I'm up to 40 pounds." Binky postured a little as if to show off her new muscles. "This weight-lifting stuff is totally awesome. I love it. Maybe I can bulk up a little. Wouldn't Harry go wild?"

"Totally wild." Todd's voice was monotone and his face expressionless.

"That's what I think too. Well, gotta go. I hate to leave you guys, but you're moving too slowly. I have to get home so I can get my homework done before Mom starts supper. If I don't watch her, that woman is apt to put fat or salt in something. I've got my dad on a low-cholesterol diet now and I think that's going to be really good for him. See ya. Bye." Binky trotted off.

"Bye, Dr. McNaughton," Lexi said as she waved. Then she turned to Todd. He was making a strange choking sound.

"Are you all right? Do you need a glass of water?" Todd's face turned bright red, but he shook his head.

"No, I'm fine. I was afraid I was going to burst out laughing, humiliate myself, and embarrass Binky. I'm glad she took off when she did. I don't think I could have held it in much longer." He laughed so hard, tears came to his eyes. Todd scrubbed at his cheek with one hand. "Binky McNaughton is bench pressing forty pounds."

"Is that good?" Lexi asked.

"Good? Lexi, the *bar* barely weighs forty pounds! Bragging about bench pressing forty pounds is a little like bragging that you can run a mile in forty-five minutes. *Everybody* should be able to do that."

"Binky never claimed to be an athlete." Lexi couldn't help smiling.

"I keep picturing it in my mind—this little tiny girl turning blue in the face trying to lift the same weights as most guys do with their little finger."

"I don't know what we'd do without Binky around Cedar River. There'd be no excitement at all, especially if she took Egg with her."

Todd and Lexi laughed as they walked, remembering the many memorable events and escapades one or the other of the McNaughtons had created. The farther they walked, however, the quieter Lexi became.

Finally Todd noticed that he was doing most of the talking. "What's wrong? Aren't the McNaughtons funny anymore?"

"I'm sorry. I'm just not in a very talkative mood."

"Do you want to tell me what's wrong?"

"My mom has another doctor's appointment today," Lexi blurted. "I can't get it out of my mind. For a few minutes I manage to forget about it and then it's back, taking center stage."

"How's she doing?"

"According to her, fine. She never complains. She acts like all those spells with her walking and her vision are no big deal. She figures that she had some sort of flu bug or virus and now it's over."

"Isn't that possible?"

"I suppose it is, but it was so *scary*, Todd. And now she acts like it never happened. She's even been doing some painting, saying her eyes aren't bothering her a bit. Sometimes, though, when she doesn't know I'm around, I catch her wearing sunglasses while she's painting on white canvas."

"Maybe she needs a good pair of glasses," Todd suggested.

"Dad told her that. It's next on her list of things to do after she gets a clean bill of health from her medical doctor."

"And none of those weird symptoms have come back?"

"No."

"Then there's probably nothing to worry about. Your mother sounds optimistic. You should be too."

"Yeah. Right."

Todd raised his eyebrow at Lexi's tone. "That's a problem?"

"I have this terrible feeling, Todd. It's so awful I shouldn't even talk about it. . . ."

"Maybe it wouldn't feel so terrible if you *did* talk."

Lexi gave him a look of anguish. "What if she dies?"

Todd blinked, startled. "What makes you think something like that?"

"I don't know. An overactive imagination, I guess. This is just all so weird and so scary. It makes me mad!"

"Mad?"

"Why can't bodies just work like they're supposed to? If God is so great, He should have made them work right!"

Lexi blushed. "Forget I said that. I have all these conflicting feelings racing around in my head. I don't know who to be mad at—Mom, the doctor, God."

"How about no one? This just happened. People get sick all the time."

"But it's not *fair*!"

"My dad says life isn't always fair. We have to deal with that."

"You're a big help," Lexi muttered.

"Sorry. I just don't want you thinking this is

someone's fault—especially God's. He's supposed to be the Guy who *helps* you! Remember?"

"You're right. I have to give Him a chance. This business has really shaken me up. I keep asking myself where my faith in God is if I'm worrying so much about Mom and not able to turn this over to Him."

"I can tell. Just remember, even if you don't feel Him in your life right now, He's going to take care of you—and your mom. He said He would. That's a good thought to hang on to."

Lexi nodded and let the conversation drop. It wouldn't do any good to discuss her mother or their family problems. It only alarmed her more because she knew that in spite of her mother's brave behavior, Mrs. Leighton was terribly, terribly frightened.

---

Supper was a quiet meal. Both Dr. and Mrs. Leighton seemed distracted. "I'll have some more salad," Lexi said.

As Mrs. Leighton picked up the bowl of mashed potatoes and passed it to Lexi, both Ben and Lexi blinked. Neither parent noticed Mrs. Leighton's mistake. Ben put down his fork and stared from one parent to the other, his dark eyes questioning.

"I'll help you clear the table, Lexi," Ben offered.

"Thanks, little guy."

Ben jumped to his feet as though relieved to be moving and carried his plate and glass into the kitchen. Ben and Lexi scraped the dishes and loaded the dishwasher. When they were done, they returned to the dining room. Dr. and Mrs. Leighton were still at the table drinking their after-dinner coffee and staring at each other with strange expressions on their faces.

"Mom? Dad?"

Mrs. Leighton started as if she hadn't even realized Lexi was in the room. "What is it, honey?"

"All that's left to go into the dishwasher are your cups."

"I'll hang on to mine a little longer," Mrs. Leighton said. "I'd like you and Benjamin to come into the living room. I want to talk to you."

Ben and Lexi exchanged still another wondering glance. Ben suddenly burst into tears.

"Benjamin, what's wrong?" His mother rubbed his back and kneeled on the floor in front of him. Huge alligator tears dripped from Benjamin's eyes and down his round pink cheeks.

"Did you hurt yourself?" Ben shook his head and wailed louder. "Lexi, what happened in the kitchen?"

"Nothing."

"Well, he surely wouldn't cry for no reason at all!"

Lexi expelled a little breath of irritation. "Mom, he's not crying for no reason! He feels the tension in this room. It's so thick, you could cut it with a knife. *That's* what's bothering him!"

Mrs. Leighton paled. "Oh. I see. I'm so sorry." Gently she took Ben's hand and led him toward the couch.

Dr. Leighton put his arm around Lexi. "Children are often sensitive to changes in household atmosphere."

"You mean," Lexi interpreted, "that Ben's feeling bad 'vibes' from you and Mom and it's frightening him."

Dr. Leighton winced. "That's exactly what I mean. I didn't realize it was quite so obvious."

"I don't know what's going on," Lexi said with a tremor in her voice, "but it's scaring me. You and Mom didn't talk at supper and Mom kept staring off into space. It's not surprising that Ben's crying. What's surprising is that *I'm* not crying too!"

"Sit down," Mrs. Leighton said softly. "We need to talk."

Dr. and Mrs. Leighton sat in the love seat, his arm draped protectively around her shoulders. Lexi perched on a chair facing them. Ben sat on the footstool at her feet.

The nerves in Lexi's body were drawn taut, like the strings on a violin.

"I went to the doctor again today. He had a diagnosis for me."

Ben blinked owlishly, not quite sure what a 'diagnosis' was, but aware that it sounded serious.

"The doctor believes I have multiple sclerosis or MS."

"What's that?" Ben wondered.

"It's a very complicated disease," Mrs. Leighton continued. "Our family has another appointment with my doctor tomorrow. He's going to talk to you and your dad, Lexi, and explain more about what he's discovered."

Before Lexi could answer, Ben burst into huge heartrending sobs.

Mrs. Leighton gathered Ben to her. She held his head against her shoulder and rocked back and forth, crooning and murmuring soothing little nonsense words in his ear. Finally the tears subsided and Ben hiccuped softly into his mother's shoulder.

"It's okay, Ben. Don't be scared. Just because the doctors found out what's wrong with me doesn't mean I'm going to change." Ben shook his head again.

Mrs. Leighton put the palms of her hands, one on either side of Ben's round face, and tilted his head until he was looking into her eyes. "Can you tell me what's wrong, Ben? What's scaring you?"

There was a potent pause before Ben choked, "Did *I* make you sick, Mommy?"

Mrs. Leighton's jaw dropped in amazement. "You? Make me sick? Of course not, Benjamin! What on earth would make you think that?"

Ben scrubbed at one eye with a fist. "If I'd been a better boy and helped out at home, would you have gotten sick?"

"What makes you think that?"

"If we help you, you don't get so tired. I don't want you to be tired anymore." Ben looked forlorn and guilty, his lower lip wobbling, his eyes welling with tears.

"Benjamin, you can't take the blame for this illness. And although it's a wonderful idea to help me around the house, that doesn't make a person well or sick. You can't take responsibility for this. I have a disease. You couldn't give me that!"

"Could too. When I've got a cold, sometimes I give it to you. And when Lexi had the stomach flu last year, she gave it to all of us, remember?"

Ben made some graphic retching sounds which, even in these intense circumstances, made the Leightons smile. "Yes, Ben, we know we got the stomach flu from Lexi. But this is different."

"Could I get . . . MS . . . too?" Ben asked. He held his stomach and looked concerned, not quite sure where this dangerous bug would reside.

"You can't catch MS, Ben. It's not like the flu. Besides, it's a disease that touches grown-ups lives, not those of little boys like you. You can be around me all day, every day, for the rest of your life and still not 'catch' multiple sclerosis."

Ben's thin shoulders relaxed. "I *can't* catch it?"

"No," Mrs. Leighton said gently. "In fact, you can give me all the kisses and hugs you want and you still won't get MS. Kisses and hugs from my kids are going to make me feel much, much better."

A smile lit Ben's features as he flung himself into his mother's arms.

"See," Mrs. Leighton laughed. "I'm feeling better already."

Ben was more easily comforted than Lexi. As she sat there in the living room watching her parents and Ben, a million thoughts raced through her mind.

*Multiple sclerosis.* She'd heard of it, of course. She thought it had to do with people in wheelchairs and she knew it was serious. What did having MS mean for her mom? What did it mean for her family? Lexi's breath caught in her throat as she wondered what would it mean for herself.

# Chapter Six

Lexi's stomach did a flip-flop as Dr. Leighton drove into the clinic parking lot. They had dropped Benjamin off at the Academy before driving downtown to the appointment with Mrs. Leighton's physician. The doctor's office was sterile and clean, decorated in pale colors and with green plants. The magazines on the coffee tables were updated, but of little interest to Lexi. She couldn't concentrate on anything. She was amazed to see how calm her mother appeared.

"Aren't you nervous?" Lexi asked her mother.

"Sometimes lately I've felt as though my insides were going to explode."

"Why don't you *look* nervous?"

"Because I'm not right now," Mrs. Leighton said honestly. "I've been frightened about the symptoms I've been having, wondering what they could be and imagining all sorts of things. Now that they have a name and a diagnosis, at least I'm not terrifying myself by thinking I have an inoperable brain tumor or something equally devastating."

"But isn't MS equally . . . devastating?" Lexi wondered.

"I don't know all the facts yet. It *is* frightening,

but at least now we have a direction to go."

"I still don't see how you can be so calm."

Mrs. Leighton smiled serenely. "You've forgotten something very important."

"What's that?"

"The same thing I'd forgotten until last evening. I've been trying to handle this on my own, Lexi. I've been attempting to be brave and strong for all of you. Last night I realized I wasn't taking advantage of the help I had available to me."

Lexi looked confused.

"I hadn't been praying! Now I've turned this whole illness over to my heavenly Father. *He* can help me get through this. I tried to do it on my own and it didn't work out. Now that I've asked Him to help me, I feel much more calm and peaceful inside. Nothing else has changed. I still have the illness. I still have to go through whatever treatment the doctor feels I need, but at least I have some peace.

"I'm ashamed to admit that I hadn't asked for help before last night. Worry had clouded my mind. I remembered the Bible verse from Psalm 22:24, 'For he has not despised or disdained the suffering of the afflicted one; he has not hidden his face from him but has listened to his cry for help.' Once I sat down and gave my problems to God, a new calmness came over me. He listened and He comforted me. I can't explain it any better than that." Mrs. Leighton put her hand on Lexi's knee. "You're going to have to do the same, Lexi, because this disease is going to be with us for a long time. We're going to need all the help we can get."

"Will the Leightons come this way, please?" The doctor was a tall, imposing man with a thatch of gray hair. He stood in the doorway, smiling at them. When Mrs. Leighton stood up, Lexi and her father followed.

Books lined two walls and pictures of his family covered the third in the doctor's consultation room.

"Good morning. It's nice to see you today." He stretched out his hand, first to Mrs. Leighton, then to Lexi, and finally to Lexi's father. "I see you're a doctor too," Dr. Klein commented.

"Of veterinary medicine. I feel a little out of my league here."

Dr. Klein chuckled. "No need to feel that way. Your patients are important too. We have a pair of golden retrievers that make our family complete."

The two doctors smiled at each other.

"Sit down. I didn't mean to keep you standing. Sometimes my mind runs ahead of my manners." He dropped into a chair behind his desk, leaned backward, and tented his fingers in front of his chin. "Now then, have you had some time to think about what I told you yesterday?"

"Frankly, I'm still in shock," Mrs. Leighton said. "I told my family last night that you believed I had multiple sclerosis, but I really didn't know what else to tell them. I'm not sure what that means for me, or for them."

"Are you sure it's MS?" Lexi's father asked. "I thought that MS was rather difficult to diagnose."

Dr. Klein nodded. "It has been in the past. Often patients go from one doctor to another, sometimes seeing as many as seven or eight, before the final MS diagnosis is made. The difficulty comes from the disease's strange variety of symptoms. Eye troubles might cause one patient to have their glasses changed. Another patient might go to a chiropractor or masseuse to alleviate other symptoms. Your wife is fortunate to have come to the right place first. MS is no longer difficult to diagnose with the proper tests. MS is marked by attacks and remissions. Symptoms can appear and disappear rather rapidly. Going to a doctor without symptoms is sometimes problematic."

"Then how can you be sure she has MS?" Lexi inquired. *Couldn't he be more specific? Her whole life was being affected by this and the doctor was rambling on about who-knows-what!* Lexi felt fear and resentment flooding through her. The emotions, raging out of control, felt as if they might consume her.

"Because of the MRI. Did your mother tell you about that?"

Lexi nodded. Things were moving too quickly for her. Her mother's disease was beginning to seem much too real.

"With the MRI, we can see MS lesions inside the body."

"Lesions?"

"That's scar tissue often found on the optic nerve, the brain stem, the spinal cord, or the cerebellum. These lesions cause numbness in the hands and feet as well as weakness and double vision.

"MS is a 'messy' disease. Its symptoms put strain on a family and then disappear for a while, often leaving its victim feeling as though everything has improved radically. That makes it a very frustrating disease, one that gives hope and then dashes it again. If you understand the nature of the disease from the onset, you're more able to prepare for both these frustrating times and happy remissions."

Dr. Leighton frowned. "Maybe it would be easier *not* to know."

Dr. Klein disagreed. "Not at all. It's very promising that your wife has had an early diagnosis. It isn't the end of the world, you know. MS *can* be managed. The sooner you learn to cope with it and get on with your lives, the better it will be for all of you."

"You really believe I can move on?" Lexi's mom looked doubtful—and hopeful.

"Definitely. I have patients who are attending school and starting new businesses. They are living full, happy lives. I can't say that MS won't change your life or that it is always easy to deal with. Still, *not* knowing you have it would only lead to more frustration and more trips to doctors. Now that we know what you have, we can not only *treat* you, but we can find ways to help you cope."

"I've been worried a lot about that lately," Mrs. Leighton admitted. "I just started to take some steps toward a career in art. I've been having trouble with my eyes and coordination. Does having MS mean that I won't be able to continue to paint?" She raked her fingers through her hair and Lexi saw that her mother's hand was trembling. "Things are just beginning to happen for me. What terrible timing this is!"

"We can't predict the course of your disease," Dr. Klein said noncommittally, "but I think you have every reason to be hopeful. There may be times, of course, when you cannot paint, or don't feel like painting. But there will be other times when you'll feel very much like doing the things you've always done. Treatment of this disease involves pacing yourself and doing what you can when you feel like doing it. If painting is a priority for you, you should be able to do it for some time to come."

"But you won't give me any guarantees," Mrs. Leighton said with a ghost of a smile.

"Guarantees are something I don't have." The doctor returned her smile. "But I do think you should be optimistic. There's no use borrowing trouble, and a good mind-set is very important."

"Can you give us a thorough explanation of what we're facing here, Dr. Klein?" Dr. Leighton's tone was businesslike but his arm rested gently around his wife's shoulders. Lexi held her mother's hand.

"Multiple sclerosis is an organic disease which affects the nervous system. While it's rarely fatal, it is progressive and, unfortunately, can cause incapacity. It seems to come and go with relapses followed by recoveries. That's why we use the term "multiple." There's really no one sign that shows itself and indicates immediately that a patient has multiple sclerosis. Any part of the nervous system can be affected—the spinal cord, the trunk, the legs, the arms. There can be numbness, tingling, or eye symptoms. Occasionally, there is also slurred speech. It is difficult to predict the degree to which patients will be affected by multiple sclerosis. Unfortunately, a few are completely paralyzed or incapacitated. Many others can carry on normal activities and work around the periods of incapacity. There are patients who are physicians, teachers, and secretaries who all lead very productive lives."

"I don't quite understand how MS does its damage," Mrs. Leighton said.

Dr. Klein nodded. "Good question. The nerve fibers in the brain and the spinal cord are covered with a sheath of myelin. In a patient with MS, this fatty sheath dissolves or disintegrates and the affected area is replaced by a scar. These scattered patches of scar tissue found throughout the nervous system are called sclerosis. Sometimes when this myelin sheath is affected, the nerve fibers are destroyed. Other times they are not. That's why the symptoms of the disease can be so erratic. Once the nerve fibers are destroyed, the nerve impulses can no longer be carried by them. That is when prolonged impairment begins."

This sounded dreadful to Lexi. She was trembling in her chair. *No!* her mind screamed. *No! No! No!*

"What can be done?"

"Building one's resistance is important. Rest is vital. I recommend that you not be exposed to extremes of hot and cold temperatures. Stay away from people with colds and the flu. A healthy lifestyle is most important. I will send you to a nutritionist so that your meals are well balanced. Take care of your body at all times. You should also remember that symptoms will usually be temporary, Mrs. Leighton, and that they will come and go.

"Frankly, the *emotional* challenges are often harder to face than the medical ones. Fear can do more harm than the disease itself." Dr. Klein pulled a sheet of paper from his file. "That's why I'd like to give you this information. There are several support groups of patients with MS in Cedar River. It's a place to share your worries with people who've been through all you may experience. This sheet has times and addresses on it and there's a self-help coordinator who can answer any questions you might have."

He smiled kindly at the family. "I've given you a lot to think about right now. In a few days you'll have many more questions. I recommend that you go home, think about what we've discussed, and talk to each other. Then, when you're ready to come back, call me and set up an appointment with my nurse and we'll talk again."

The doctor turned to Lexi. "Do *you* have any questions you'd like answered right now?"

He'd taken her by surprise. Lexi knew she had a *million* questions—but at the moment her mind felt totally blank. "I . . . uh . . ."

"It's not easy for a young lady like yourself to hear this," the doctor said. "I know that when you get home, you'll wish you'd received more answers. I'd like you to write down any questions you might have over the next few days and either bring them back to me or send them with your parents. MS is a disease that the entire family suffers. You are a part of this too. You can help to ease the difficulties your mother may face, or you can add to the problem. I'd rather help you see ways to do the former. We're a team now—you, your parents, and me. We've got a formidable opponent in MS, but it doesn't have to win."

Dr. Klein took Mrs. Leighton's hands in his own and looked into her eyes. Lexi could see his compassion and affection there.

"Just remember, you're still in charge of your

life. This disease does not have to take over. It's not in control, *you* are. Learning all you can, taking care of yourself, and dealing with the emotional aspects of MS are your first jobs."

Mrs. Leighton nodded numbly. The family stood up and after shaking hands with the doctor, left his office.

"Well, now what?" Lexi asked.

"I think we should go to the library," Mrs. Leighton suggested. "If I'm supposed to learn what I can about this disease, I want to start today."

"Do you feel up to it?" Dr. Leighton asked.

"I'm *not* going to sit around and wait to feel ill so I can feel sorry for myself."

---

There were dozens of books on multiple sclerosis on the library shelves.

"How are we ever going to read all these?" Lexi wondered as she and her mother and father staggered to the car under their load of books.

"We'll get through them," Dr. Leighton said. "Right now we're a highly motivated family, don't you think?" He glanced at his watch. "It's almost noon. Is anyone interested in lunch?"

"I'm not very hungry," Lexi said.

Mrs. Leighton dropped her books into the backseat of the car. "But I am. I want a burger and fries and a chocolate malt."

Lexi looked at her mother in surprise. "Mom, you never eat like that!"

"I know, but today I'm celebrating."

"Celebrating?"

Mrs. Leighton nodded. "I don't have a terminal

disease. I have one that needs to be managed. Right now, that's good news. I believe we have something to celebrate."

At the restaurant, Mrs. Leighton seemed almost giddy, as though the meeting in the doctor's office had not occurred. Lexi was relieved to see her mother smiling.

"You know," Mrs. Leighton said as she leaned back in the booth at the restaurant and waved a french fry in the air, "I'm wondering if that doctor was wrong after all." Lexi and Dr. Leighton stared at her.

"What do you mean?"

"It's possible, you know, that he read the tests incorrectly. I don't think I have something as serious as MS. I don't feel that sick. I probably need glasses and a lot more rest. But MS—don't you think that's pretty farfetched?" She dipped the french fry in the ketchup on her plate and popped it into her mouth. "I wonder if I should look for another doctor? Dr. Klein's very nice but . . ."

Her husband shook his head adamantly. "Don't do this, Marilyn."

"Don't do what?"

"Deny what you've been told."

"I'm not in denial, Jim. I'm just wondering if that doctor really knows what he's talking about. He gave me a prescription for some medication, but I'm not sure I need to take it."

"You can't do this to yourself or to us." Dr. Leighton was very stern. "We've had a lot of shocks this week. You haven't been sick very long and you received your diagnosis very quickly. You were on the right track at the library earlier, Marilyn. The best way to get over this shock is to learn as much about MS as possible and to learn it quickly. It's one thing to refuse to think about your disease every day or to dwell on it when you can't do anything about it. It's quite another to deny you have it."

Mrs. Leighton grew very quiet. The animation that had lit her features disappeared.

"I don't want to rain on your parade, but we've got to deal with this, sweetheart. Denying it is not going to make it go away." Lexi's father was firm.

Mrs. Leighton was silent for a long time. Lexi watched her parents, holding her breath. Finally a tear leaked from beneath one of Mrs. Leighton's lids.

"Maybe you're right. It just felt so good to think that doctor was wrong. . . ."

"But I don't believe he is wrong, and you don't either. Denial isn't going to do you any good."

Mrs. Leighton nodded stoically. "You're right, of course. If I do have this disease, I have to face it. Nothing else will work."

---

"Does anyone have an answer to question twenty-four?"

Binky, Peggy, Lexi, and Jennifer were studying together at Binky's house.

"Binky, you don't need help with that one too! We've helped you with questions one through twenty-three."

"I had most of the answers right, didn't I?"

"Yes."

"I just want to get a *perfect* paper. Don't you think that would surprise my teacher?"

"That would surprise everyone, Binky."

Lexi couldn't concentrate. The others were chattering about school and classes. Her world was falling apart and all they could talk about was history and math and . . .

"Lexi, are you all right?" Peggy peered into Lexi's eyes. "You look awfully pale. You've been very quiet tonight. Are you feeling okay?"

"I'm feeling fine. . . ." Lexi choked, paused, and burst into sobs. Jennifer, Peggy, and Binky surrounded her like mother hens, clucking and patting her shoulders helplessly, asking what was wrong and what they could do. When Lexi's tears subsided she took the wad of tissue Binky held out to her.

"What happened? What did we say?"

"You didn't say anything."

"Then why are you crying?"

Lexi looked into the faces of her friends and knew she couldn't keep her secret any longer. "My mom's sick. Really sick. And I don't know what to do. My whole world is falling apart and I don't know how to stop it!"

"What's wrong with your mom?" Jennifer asked.

"She's got MS—multiple sclerosis."

"Oh, I've heard of that. Isn't that when people have to sit in wheelchairs. . . ?" Binky slapped her hand over her mouth. "Never mind."

"That's right, Bink. Sometimes people *do* end up in wheelchairs. Not always, though." Lexi told her friends all she'd learned from the doctor and from the books she and her family had been studying. "The doctor says that she may be just fine for a long, long time. Maybe even forever. But I can't quit worrying. What if she gets really sick? What if she can't take care of us anymore? What if she can't paint? What if she has to be in a nursing home? What am I going to do?"

The questions were bitter on Lexi's tongue. For the first time she understood that fear had a taste. Even the thought of her mother in a nursing home—like Grandma—gave Lexi a chill. She was too young! Too vital! And Lexi and Ben *needed* her!

"Is MS catchy?"

Lexi spun to stare at Binky.

A look of horror crossed Binky's features. "I'm sorry. I shouldn't have said that."

"Do you mean, could you catch it from my mom?" Lexi asked, voice trembling.

Binky hung her head. "It was very selfish of me, Lexi. I'm sorry I asked."

Gathering every bit of control she could muster, Lexi answered, "They think MS is a virus, but it's not catchy in the same way a cold is catchy. People can live together their whole lives and one can have MS and the other will never get it. I guess that means you don't have to worry about coming over to the house, Binky."

"I feel horrible," Binky said. "I'm vain and I'm self-centered. The first thing I thought about was myself when you were telling me about your mother and the trouble your family was having." Tears came to her eyes. "This self-improvement thing has gone too far."

"What does that have to do with anything?" Jennifer asked sharply.

"My best friend in the world is having trouble and I'm worrying about myself and how it will affect *me*. I'm thinking too much about me and not enough about others." Binky put her arm around Lexi's shoulders. "And I'm going to quit that right now. Lexi has a problem and we have to be here for her."

Peggy and Jennifer nodded. "Binky's right, Lexi. We're here for you."

Lexi closed her eyes and gave a watery sigh. "I'm glad." She wasn't going to be able to handle this alone.

---

"How are things going?" Lexi greeted her mother as she entered the back door after school. Mrs. Leighton was seated at the counter, going through some papers that Lexi had left for her that morning.

"When did this bulletin from school come?"

Lexi averted her eyes. She went to the refrigerator and pulled out a carton of juice. "Oh, maybe yesterday or the day before."

"Why didn't I get it until today?" Mrs. Leighton wondered.

"I must have forgotten it in my book bag. I've got a lot of junk in there that I should clean out. Maybe I'll do that after school. I don't have much homework and . . ."

"I see that there was a PTA meeting last night."

"Really? I guess I didn't notice."

"I don't believe that, honey. You made notes on this sheet of paper. Why didn't you tell me? You know I *always* go to PTA meetings."

"I just missed it, Mom. It's no big deal. You say yourself that most of those PTA meetings are a real drag."

"Did you neglect to tell me because you were embarrassed to have me there?" Mrs. Leighton's gaze was piercing. Lexi wanted to disappear.

"Lexi, are you going to answer me?"

Lexi was silent for a long time. "I don't have anything to say."

"I was right, then, wasn't I? You *didn't* want me at the PTA meeting. That's why I got this notice this morning instead of yesterday."

Lexi hung her head. She placed the juice on the counter and squeezed her eyes tightly shut. Tears formed behind the lids. "I didn't think you'd want to go. All those people and that big crowd. Sometimes you stumble. . . ."

"And you're embarrassed by it," Mrs. Leighton finished the sentence for her.

Lexi's cheeks burned and her heart pounded in her chest. She felt so ashamed. It wasn't until she felt her mother's hand on her arm that Lexi was able to open her eyes.

"It's all right, Lexi. I understand."

"How could you? *I* don't understand. I saw that note in the bulletin and I was going to bring it home. Then I thought about you having trouble walking and all those people staring at you and—I just couldn't tell you, Mom. I just couldn't."

"Teenagers are self-conscious about the way their parents dress, the uncool things they say, and the antiquated ways they think. Lexi, I've embarrassed you even *before* I was diagnosed with MS. Sometimes I wonder if that isn't part of my job description. More than once you've suggested I change clothes because the ones I was wearing didn't look cool enough for you."

"I'm sorry. That was selfish of me."

"No, that's just being a teenager. I've never minded. I *want* to look nice. I *want* to make you proud of me when I go out in public. But this limp of mine may be here to stay. I might stumble once in awhile. I may come to the point where I need a cane. I can accept that as long as I don't have to be trapped in my own home. You'll have to realize that."

"I feel so ashamed. I didn't think it through. I was worried about being embarrassed."

"I understand why you'd feel awkward about having a mom who can't walk a straight line. I remember the look on your face the day Binky asked me if I was drunk. It was pretty hard to take. Not just at your age, but at any age."

"I wish you could trade me in and get a daughter who is better. Someone you deserve." She felt like a traitor. Benedict Arnold in blue jeans. Lexi wondered what kind of a person she'd become.

"Give yourself a break, Lexi. Teenagers are naturally embarrassed by a lot of things. I've seen you fuss about going to school with a pimple on your chin, so it's hardly any wonder that you're bothered by this! Unfortunately, you're going to have to start thinking of your mom as one great big pimple." Mrs. Leighton poked Lexi in the side with her finger hoping to elicit a smile. It didn't work. Lexi refused to be cajoled into good humor.

"I'm so ashamed. I can't believe I ever thought that way. What's wrong with me?" Lexi curled her shoulders forward miserably.

"You're human. That's what's wrong with all of us. My illness will be hard on everyone. We're going to have to work it out together, as a family. The only way I can get through this is with the strength that you, your dad, and Ben can give me. I know it won't always be smooth sailing, but we love each other enough not to let this get in the way of what we feel for one another. We just hit a bumpy spot today, that's all.

"Next time something bothers you, talk about it. Get it out in the open. We'll do some problem solving. Find a solution. We'll make it. I know we will."

"I'm not so sure, Mom. I'm really scared this time."

Mrs. Leighton put her arms around Lexi. "We're doing it again, Lexi. We're not tapping into the source of strength that will help us get through anything. 'The LORD is my rock, my fortress and my deliverer; my God is my rock, in whom I take refuge. He is my shield and my stronghold.' Have you been praying?"

Lexi hung her head. "Not like I should. Lately, it feels as though my heart hurts. It's hard to pray."

"That's when you need it most," Mrs. Leighton said.

"But I don't feel like God is listening. If He were, you wouldn't be sick!"

"He's listening, all right." Mrs. Leighton ruffled her daughter's hair. "That's one thing I've learned. God never moves away from us. Only we can move away from Him. Sometimes when you pray, you have to do so even though it may feel as though there's no one 'there.' Faith is more than a feeling."

"Good, because I'm not crazy about the way I'm feeling right now." And Lexi wasn't sure she was ever going to feel good again.

---

"Mom, I'm going over to Binky's. Do you need anything at the store?"

Mrs. Leighton was in her studio sketching. "No, thanks. I'm just fine."

Lexi peeked over her mother's shoulder. "That looks great."

"I know. I'm really in the mood today and I'm feeling good, so I'm having a lot of fun. I think I'll do a pen and ink series next. I haven't done that for a long time."

"I'm glad to see you working."

"Why are you going to Binky's?"

"Another self-improvement meeting."

"Binky never gives up, does she?"

"I guess that's the best and the worst thing about Binky."

Mrs. Leighton took Lexi's hand. "And pretty soon you're going to be saying that about me. I'm not giving up either."

Lexi kissed her mom on the forehead and left for the McNaughtons.

"I'm glad you're here," Binky greeted Lexi at the door. "I wanted to apologize again for being so vain and self-centered the other day."

"Forget it."

"My self-improvement plan seems really stupid when your family has such big things to face. Maybe I should just call it quits."

"Don't. I think it's *important* that you keep on."

"You do?" Binky looked startled by the sincerity in Lexi's voice.

"Since my mom's illness I've started to realize

how important it is to take care of yourself. Most of what Mom has to do is to rest, eat good meals, and avoid stress. The doctor says she has to keep her spirits up as well as her strength. That's self-improvement too. If we could learn to do that early in our lives, it would be a whole lot better for us."

Binky looked cheered at the thought. "You really think so?"

"Absolutely. Don't give up on this self-improvement thing. You're on the right track."

"Thanks, Lexi. You've made me feel a lot better." Binky straightened and her eyes brightened. "You mean doctors are telling people to do the things that I'm doing?"

"Absolutely."

"Well then," Binky said, a proud look spreading across her face. "Maybe my little self-improvement idea isn't so bad after all!"

# Chapter Seven

"Egg and I are going to the Hamburger Shack," Todd said. "Do you want to come along?"

"You haven't been there with us for a long time," Egg observed. "Besides, we have something to celebrate."

"What's that?"

"We're getting out of school two hours early!"

"Thanks for the invitation, but I think I'll pass this time. My mom planned to paint all day. I'd like to go home to talk her into taking a break. She works too hard."

"I read the article about her in the newspaper," Todd said. "Impressive. The reporter called her Cedar River's 'shining new talent.' "

"Mom framed that article. It's hanging in her studio." Lexi glanced at her watch. "I'd better get going. Thanks for the offer. Next time, all right?"

Lexi pulled the car into the Leighton's driveway and turned the key in the ignition. It would be over an hour before someone would have to pick Benjamin up from school at the Academy for the Handicapped.

The back door was unlocked and the kitchen was quiet. Lexi opened the refrigerator and took out a can of soda. She popped the top and reached for a bag of potato chips which she carried down the hall to her mother's studio.

"Mom, are you here?"

The door was shut. Music was blaring from the studio. This surprised Lexi. Her mother normally played muted classical sounds, the type she said inspired her the most. This heavy metal music was totally unlike anything Lexi's mother was accustomed to playing.

Mrs. Leighton was seated with her back to the door, facing her easel. She was painting in large angry strokes with bright unmixed, undiluted colors.

Perhaps "painting" wasn't the right word, Lexi realized with alarm. Her mother was jabbing angrily at the canvas in jerky thrusts. It was more like swordfighting with brush and canvas.

Lexi could see from the corner of the canvas that this had once been a floral piece on which her mother had spent a great deal of time. The flowers were now mostly hidden by bright angry jags of paint. Other canvases sat on the floor nearby. All had suffered the same alarming fate.

"Mom?" Lexi stepped hesitantly into the room. Mrs. Leighton didn't hear her. Lexi walked over to the stereo and turned down the volume. Mrs. Leighton's shoulders jerked and she spun around on her stool, her eyes flashing.

"Who did that? Oh, Lexi. What are you doing here?" She glanced dazedly at the clock on the wall. "School isn't out yet. Why are you home?"

"We were dismissed early. The teachers had an in-service. They forgot to put it on the school calendar. I didn't know about it myself until I got to school this morning."

"That's nice." Mrs. Leighton seemed confused trying to make a shift from one thought process to another. The painting behind her with its angry streaks of color was a strange contrast to the soft voice with which she spoke to her daughter.

Lexi walked over to the easel and pointed to the canvas. "I loved that floral. What have you done to it?"

"It simply wasn't working. The colors were insipid and I didn't like the balance. I thought I could fix it up, but then I got frustrated so I just started painting."

"And those?" Lexi pointed to the canvases on the floor.

"I don't know where my mind was when I was painting these pictures," Mrs. Leighton said. "They were very weak. I didn't like any of them. I thought I'd brighten them up."

"I heard you tell Dad these were some of your very best works."

"I don't know what I was thinking. I looked at them today and they made me so angry. I don't even know what made me think I could paint!" Mrs. Leighton swept her hand toward the picture and knocked the canvas off the easel. It tumbled to the floor landing faceup. Lexi had never seen her mother in a mood like this and it terrified her.

Mrs. Leighton stared for a long time at the painting lying on the floor, then her shoulders drooped, her head fell into her hands, and she began to cry heartrending sobs that tore at Lexi's insides. Without another word, Lexi hurried to the phone in the kitchen and called her father.

"Dad, you've got to come home. Something's wrong with mom."

"What's happened, Lexi? Has she fallen?"

"No, she's crying, ruining her paintings and she's playing loud music. I don't understand."

"I'll be right there."

Lexi returned to the studio to attempt to comfort her mother, but Mrs. Leighton continued to cry. Lexi was relieved to hear the back door open and her father's footsteps coming down the hall. Dr. Leighton looked over the room, saw the angry pictures, and asked gently, "Okay honey, what's going on here?"

Marilyn Leighton looked upward through her tears. "I tried to paint. I wanted to finish these today. My hand kept shaking and my vision kept changing. I couldn't *do* it! I couldn't copy my *own* style! Do you know how frightened, frustrated, and angry that makes me? Whatever made me think I could paint anyway? Not now, not with this diagnosis. Just when my career has finally taken a tiny step forward, this happens. . . ." She held out a trembling hand.

"You're angry?" Dr. Leighton asked softly.

"Angry? I'm *furious*. I'm *livid*. There aren't even words to express what I feel! I've waited years for the kids to be independent so that I could spend more time on my paintings. Lexi's doing well in school. Ben loves his classes at the Academy. Now should be my time, *my* time. This stupid disease doesn't fit into the plan I had for my life."

She thrust the brush she was holding into a glass jar.

"Maybe that's what I get for making plans. I had hopes. I had dreams. I had ambitions. Now everything is ruined."

Lexi had never heard her mother speak this way. The ring of bitterness and of truth was chilling.

Dr. Leighton, however, looked neither terrified nor surprised. He moved to his wife and helped her off the stool and into a more comfortable chair. "Of course you're angry. I'd think there would be something wrong with you if you weren't."

Mrs. Leighton was surprised by her husband's response. "What do you mean?"

"Think about it," he said. "You've just learned that you have a disease that could be either very serious or could be of little consequence. You have no idea when the disease is going to flare up or how it will affect you. You'll have to learn to live with it, and there's nothing else you can do. You have every right to be angry."

"I do?"

"Of course," Dr. Leighton said gently. "Everything seems changed right now. All the plans, all the hopes, all the dreams you've ever had all seem to be in jeopardy. But they *aren't*. We just don't know which ones you're going to achieve yet, that's all. As bad as this disease can be, it can also be very mild. The frustrating part is that you don't know which it will be or when it will happen."

"Sometimes I feel so angry, I could just scream."

"Then maybe you should."

Both Lexi and her mother stared at Dr. Leighton in surprise. "If you feel like screaming, do it," he said emphatically. "Go into our bedroom. Take a pillow, put it over your mouth. Scream until your throat is raw. You deserve it. After all, this disease has come along and messed up your plans—our plans. I feel like screaming sometimes too. You have to ventilate. You're just like a pressure cooker that's ready to let off steam. You have to let off *some* anger. If you can't scream, cry." Dr. Leighton's expression was intense.

"I've thought about it a lot, Marilyn. I know how brave you're trying to be. I'm trying to be brave for you too, but do you know what? I think instead of bravery what we need is a little old-fashioned *grieving*. No one in this family needs to bury their feelings. More than once in the past few days I've felt like throwing things or punching my hand into the wall. It's a reaction that has some merit. We have to get these feelings out. We all need to blow off a little steam, honey. It's all right to do this to your paintings. You're not angry at your paintings. You're angry at the MS, that's all. Know what you're angry at and get it out of your system."

"I feel so out of control."

Dr. Leighton nodded, his eyes compassionate. "But you can be the one in charge, Marilyn. Take it. Get rid of your anger so that you can do all the other things you need to do, like learning to cope with this disease you have. You're strong, brave, and wonderful. This disease won't get the best of you unless you let it."

A flicker of hope seemed to spring into Mrs. Leighton's eyes. "You think so? You *really* think so?"

"Without a doubt. Don't be afraid of your feelings. Accept them, deal with them, and move on."

Dr. Leighton opened his arms, and his wife

walked into them, crying softly. Lexi stood at their side for a moment, not quite knowing what to do. Then instinctively she did the thing that seemed most right. She walked into the circle of their arms where the three of them stood hugging and crying.

---

"But I don't *want* to go out for lunch!" Lexi protested as Binky, Peggy, and Jennifer towed her toward the Food Court at the mall.

"Sure you do. You just don't realize it. You've been cooped up in the house for days. This will be good for you."

"I'm not hungry."

"You will be. Binky, you stay here with Lexi. Peggy and I will pick up something to eat."

After Jennifer and Peggy had left, Lexi sighed and leaned back in the molded plastic chair. "I know what you guys are up to, you know."

"What's that?" Binky asked innocently.

"Diversion. You're trying to distract me so that I won't worry about Mom."

"And what's wrong with that?"

"Nothing—except that it's not working. No matter what I do, I can't quit worrying about her."

"Let us help you," Binky responded. "We're feeling as helpless as you are right now."

Lexi gave her friend an appreciative smile. Before she could speak, Peggy and Jennifer arrived with the food.

"Pizza all around!" Peggy said. "Pepperoni, Italian sausage, Canadian bacon and pineapple. What kind do you want?" She dealt out slices of pizza around the table. When she got to Binky, she paused. "What's wrong with you?"

"Do you know how many fat grams there are in a slice of pizza?" Binky ventured.

"Don't think about that today! Besides, we brought diet soft drinks. No calories. It will even out."

Binky pursed her lips disapprovingly but took a slice of pizza. Carefully she unfolded a napkin and pressed it against the top of the pizza.

"What are you doing?"

Binky lifted the napkin, now stained with oil. "Blotting off the excess fat. See?"

Jennifer made a gagging sound as she stared at the yellowed napkin. "That's so gross."

"It's more gross in your arteries," Binky said primly. Then she picked up her pizza and began to eat.

Lexi burst out laughing. "You did it!" The other three girls stared at her wonderingly.

"Did what?"

"Made me forget about my mom for a minute. It felt great. Thanks, guys." Giggling and shaking her head, Lexi bit into her pizza.

"Weird. Definitely weird," Binky concluded. No one knew who she was talking about—herself or them.

---

Lexi tiptoed up the stairs and down the hallway to her mother's room. The door was slightly ajar and Lexi peeked inside. The shades were drawn, encasing the bedroom in an aura of gloom. There were discarded clothes cast over chairs and the dressing table. Through the duskiness, Lexi could see her mother curled into a fetal position in the center of the bed. She was asleep, again . . . as usual.

Lexi couldn't remember how many days it had been since she'd come home from school and found her mother in the kitchen or the studio working. Instead, Mrs. Leighton slept a great deal, as though through sleeping she could escape the reality of her diagnosis. Lexi chewed for a moment on her lower lip before coming to a decision. She pushed open the door, then strode into the room and over to the bed.

"Mom, it's me, Lexi. I'm home."

"I'm napping, Lexi. Talk to me later."

"What time did you lie down?" Lexi persisted.

"I don't know . . . noon, one o'clock. I'm still tired."

"You've rested for almost four hours. Why don't you get up now? I'll bet some exercise would feel good. We could go for a walk."

"I don't want to walk."

"Then we could go for a bike ride. It's a beautiful afternoon."

"I don't want to go for a bike ride either, Lexi. Later. Just leave me alone now, please."

Lexi did everything she could to cajole her mother out of bed, but it was no good. Mrs. Leighton refused to budge. She clamped a pillow over her face and her arm over the pillow until Lexi wasn't even sure her mother could hear her talking. With tears welling in her eyes, Lexi backed out of the bedroom and moved toward the stairs.

*I can't take it anymore.*

The way her mother was behaving terrified her. Even though Lexi's father had assured Lexi that depression was not abnormal in circumstances such as these, it was difficult to accept it when it was her own mother curled in the center of a bed refusing to move. Suddenly the air in the house felt very close and tight. Lexi had to escape.

Lexi hurried into the sunlight. Not knowing or caring where she was going Lexi started out, her arms swinging, her hair blowing in the afternoon breeze. Her feet carried her as fast as they could. Walking hard and fast felt mindless and cleansing. The deep breaths of air she took purged her body of some of the anxiety she was feeling. When Lexi finally stopped to look at a street sign, she was surprised to find herself only one block from her family's church. Intuitively, Lexi had the sensation that God was trying to tell her something if only she would listen. She glanced toward the church and saw Pastor Lake's car alone in the parking lot. Lexi turned and strode toward the church.

"Hello, Lexi. What are you doing here today?" Pastor Lake looked up from his exceedingly messy desk, stretched his arms over his head, and gave a big yawn. "I'm trying to compose a brilliant sermon for Sunday church, but I'm not feeling particularly brilliant right now. Come in and sit down. Talk to me."

"I was out walking," Lexi said. "I didn't plan to come here, but when I realized where I was, it was only a block from the church. I decided that maybe this was the place I was supposed to come."

Pastor Lake looked mildly curious, but not surprised. "And what do you think you were to find here?"

"I don't know. You, maybe . . . answers . . . help."

"How's your mother doing? Is she feeling better?" Pastor Lake went right to the heart of the matter.

"Yes and no. She hasn't had any serious MS symptoms lately. My dad says she is suffering from depression. She wants to sleep all the time. She pulls the curtains and curls into a ball on the couch or on her bed and falls asleep. I've tried to get her up but she refuses. Dad says it's not surprising considering the shock she's had recently, but it's scaring me."

Pastor Lake nodded thoughtfully. "I think your dad's right. It seems normal that your mother would be depressed about the news she's received."

"But what can we do about it? I can't stand to see Mom lying there. She isn't painting. She doesn't cook. She's not interested in playing games with Ben and me. Sometimes she just sits and stares at the wall."

"Your mother is grieving, Lexi. She's grieving for the loss of her health and her life as she knows it. Perhaps there is no other way for her to get over this period in her life than to go through it. Maybe the best thing you can do is to stay with her, tell her that you love her, and just stare at the wall with her."

"Shouldn't she go to the doctor and get some pills or something?"

"I would predict that your mother is going to start feeling emotionally stronger soon. She's a very independent and resourceful woman. She's going to snap out of this, but not until she's ready. Your mom has lots of things to work through right now, Lexi. We all have to give her a chance to do that."

"What if she doesn't 'snap out of it'?" Lexi's voice was shaky with fear. "I don't think I can stand this much longer, Pastor Lake."

"It would be wise for your father and mother to talk to her doctor about this situation. Perhaps he can suggest some counseling or medication to get her through this difficult time. But your mother's a strong, vital woman. Sooner or later she's going to shed this depression and move on to the next step in this process."

"And what step is that?" Lexi wondered.

"Acceptance. Humans are amazingly resilient. What's more, your mother has a deep and abiding faith in God. One of the most important things you can do for her right now—and for yourself—is to pray." Pastor Lake reached for his Bible. "Let's look up some verses right now that might help you or that you can share with your mom."

He opened the Bible to 1 Peter 2:24. "This is one of my personal favorites. 'He himself bore our sins in his body on the tree, so that we might die to sins and live for righteousness; by his wounds you have been healed.' "

He tapped the page with the tip of his pen. "If God can heal us of the sin that permeates our lives, then He can certainly heal our bodily illnesses!"

"I never thought of it that way."

" 'The LORD is good, a refuge in times of trouble. He cares for those who trust in him,' Nahum 1:7. That's the secret, Lexi. Trust. Faith. Dependence upon God. That's what will carry your family through this crisis.

"I hope so," Lexi said wistfully, "because we need all the help we can get."

---

"I'm glad you came down for supper, mom," Lexi said. They were all seated around the dinner table. Lexi and Benjamin had prepared the meal as they had done so often in the past week.

"I love macaroni and cheese," Ben announced, eyeing the casserole in the middle of the table.

"And hot dogs and hamburgers," Mrs. Leighton added.

"And soup out of a can," Ben finished for his mother.

"You two are very good cooks and I appreciate your efforts, but I think it's time I started making a few meals around here. I don't want to put all the responsibility on your shoulders."

Lexi brightened. It was the most normal Mrs. Leighton had sounded in many days.

"I know I haven't been much good to my family lately," Mrs. Leighton continued. "I've been feeling sorry for myself. Your dad says I'm depressed, and I'm afraid he's right."

"What's depressed?" Ben stirred the macaroni around on his plate, making little patterns in the cheese.

"I don't like the fact that I have MS and it's making me sad. I don't want to be sick. It's hard for me to accept that I am."

Ben looked at his mother thoughtfully. "You think something's wrong with you because you're different from everybody else."

"I suppose you could say that. I have a disease that most people don't have."

Ben looked at his mother. "It's *okay* to be different, Mother."

Mrs. Leighton blinked, startled. "What?"

"I've got Down's syndrome and *I'm* okay. You've got MS and you're okay too. We don't all have to be the same to be good. You said that people being different from each other is what makes life 'interesting.' That makes me and you really interesting, Mom."

Mrs. Leighton stared at her son as if she were seeing him for the very first time. Ben's round face and almond-shaped eyes were glowing. His silky brown hair fell in a shaggy thatch over his forehead. He was as sweet and beautiful and beguiling looking as Lexi could ever remember seeing him.

"Out of the mouths of babes," Mrs. Leighton said, shaking her head.

"I'm no baby!" Ben's expression flickered for a moment.

"Of course you aren't! That's not what I meant." Mrs. Leighton smiled broadly at her son. "What I meant was, sometimes the brightest, most intelligent, most perceptive words come out of the mouth of a child. You're absolutely, *one hundred percent* correct, Benjamin.

"If I don't believe that I'm okay as a human being just because I have MS, then I'm not practicing what I've been preaching. Just because I'm not physically perfect, I'm still a good person. I'm still your mom. I can still paint on the days that I'm not too tired. And I'm still the wife of the best husband and veterinarian in the entire world."

"Thata girl, Mom," Ben cheered.

Mrs. Leighton wiped a tear out of the corner of her eye with her napkin. "I don't know why I didn't see this before," she admitted. "*Disabilities do not diminish the person.* That's what I say to others who ask what it's like to have a challenged child. Disabilities change a person, certainly, but I'm no less valuable with MS than I would be without it! That would be like saying you're less precious because you have Down's syndrome, Ben."

Mrs. Leighton stood up and walked around the table to hug her young son. "Thank you for making me see what I couldn't discover on my own."

"It's okay, Mom. I'll help anytime you need it." Ben went back to eating his macaroni and cheese.

Lexi exchanged a secret smile with her father. Her heart was soaring. For the first time in many days, she had a sense that things could be all right again in the Leighton household.

---

Mrs. Leighton was already frying bacon and mixing up a batch of pancake batter when Lexi entered the kitchen the next morning. Her hair was combed and she was singing. She looked better than she had in days.

"Good morning, darling. Pancakes? They're almost ready."

"I guess I have time. It's great to see you downstairs, Mom."

"I have to apologize to you and to your dad and to Ben. I've been behaving very badly. It's time for me to get a grip on myself and to get on with my life!" Mrs. Leighton sounded determined and enthusiastic.

"Did Ben make all these changes happen?" Lexi wondered.

Mrs. Leighton smiled. "I was coming around already, Lexi, but he's the one who made the final pieces of the puzzle fall into place. I've spent my whole life trying to teach people that disabilities do not diminish a person. And when something comes along that might be a disability for me, what's the first thing I do? Fall apart. Ironic, isn't it? Just because I have MS doesn't mean I've received a death sentence!" Mrs. Leighton sounded a little awed by the realization.

"Actually, I feel wonderful right now, better than I have in a long time. I have to be optimistic. My MS might be mild. Or maybe someone will discover a cure by the time I really need it. I can't quit looking forward to the future just because I *might* become sick. If I need to rest more than I can paint, so be it. I will paint as much as possible while I can enjoy it."

Mrs. Leighton moved around the counter and embraced her daughter. "I'm going to have to turn this disease over to God, Lexi. I can't worry about the future. It ruins the present."

"Isn't it going to be hard?"

"I imagine it will be. That's why I'm planning to attend the 'Living With MS' group that my doctor has recommended. It meets this evening." A look of hesitancy crossed Mrs. Leighton's features. "I think it's going to be very hard to go for the first time, admitting publicly that something's wrong with me." She squared her shoulders. "I guess I'll just have to do it."

"Would you like me to go with you?" Lexi offered.

"You'd do that for me?"

"Sure. You've got MS. I'm going to have to learn about it too. I'd be glad to come."

Mrs. Leighton reached out to hug her daughter again. "Thank you, Lexi. It means a great deal to me."

---

The "Living With MS" meeting was held in a small room in the basement of the Cedar River Hospital. Lexi's stomach was churning and her palms were sweaty as she and her mother walked into the room. What she had expected, Lexi didn't know, but it certainly wasn't this.

A group of perfectly normal-looking people were milling around drinking coffee, laughing, and exchanging jokes. There was no one here who looked sick.

In the corner there were three people in wheelchairs pulled up to a card table playing a game, but they didn't look depressed by the fact they were in wheelchairs. Two others had canes but they used them so naturally and without self-consciousness that at first she hadn't even realized they had them.

What *had* she expected? Pale, despondent-looking people with hollow eyes. And what had she found? A group of nice, normal-looking people, some of whom were dependent on wheelchairs and canes. Others had no signs of sickness whatsoever. This could have been a meeting for the parent-teacher association or a committee at church. A burden lifted from Lexi's heart.

Her mother was not going to change just because she had MS. She was still going to be Mom. She might have to depend on a wheelchair or cane someday, but then again, maybe not. Lexi would think about that when the time came. These people had discovered they had MS and survived. Mrs. Leighton could too.

A tall, attractive woman stood up and clapped her hands. "I think we're all here now," she said. "If you'll take your places, we'll go around the circle and introduce ourselves. After that we'll continue our discussion from last week."

That discussion turned out to be near and dear to Mrs. Leighton's and Lexi's heart. Acceptance.

"What are more ways that we can know we truly have accepted our disease and are willing to move on with our lives?" Mrs. Janzen asked.

"At first I found it very difficult to accept help from others," a woman with gray hair in a wheelchair said. "I always turned down offers of help for things I couldn't do myself because I didn't know how I could repay all those gracious offers."

"And now?" Mrs. Janzen prodded.

"Now when someone does something kind for me, like shovel my walk or bring me a home-cooked meal, I find something I can do for them. I'm a wonderful crocheter and I've made a lot of doilies as gifts to people who've been Good Samaritans to me. The young gentleman who shovels my walk has made a deal with me. He keeps the snow off my sidewalk and I mend all the rips and tears in his clothing. He can't sew and I can't use the shovel, so we need each other. I don't turn down help anymore. I just find ways to say thank you."

"I started to accept my disease when I began to go to the beauty shop again," an attractive woman in her fifties piped. "After I learned about my diagnosis, I didn't care about anything. I didn't fix my hair, polish my nails, or put on makeup. I wore the same outfit day after day. My personal hygiene deteriorated. When I realized that this was going to be my life from now on, I finally accepted the fact that I had to deal with MS instead of moping about. I made an appointment at the beauty shop. I had my hair colored and permed and I got a new hairstyle." The lady patted her hairdo fondly. "And I like it very much. It makes me look younger, don't you think?"

"All right!" someone cheered from the other side of the room. "I think you look great!"

"That's a wonderful point," Mrs. Janzen said. "You've got to have a positive self-image. We have to take care of ourselves. We need to rest when we have to rest, eat the proper food, get the proper exercise. Know what works for us and know what doesn't. When you start to do those things, I believe you've accepted your MS and you're on to a healthy life.

"For a while, I blamed all the troubles in my life on my disease," Mrs. Janzen admitted. "I felt my MS was responsible for everything—even the dishwasher breaking down. When I quit accusing the disease of causing all my problems, I felt a lot better about myself and the world around me."

"I think the best thing I ever did was come to this group," a gentleman spoke up. His hair was crisp and dark and he looked the picture of health. "I don't want to discuss my disease at work and I don't think my co-workers want to hear about it either. Knowing that I can come here once a week and talk to people who have the same problems gives me strength and encouragement. And it's also an outlet." Turning to Mrs. Leighton, "That's why we're so glad you're here, Marilyn. You're going to learn a lot from us, and we expect to learn a lot from you."

---

"Weren't those people nice, Mom?" Lexi said enthusiastically on the trip home.

"They were wonderful. I feel more optimistic than I have in weeks. Now I have some people to talk to—people who can help me through the 'down' days when I need a boost. Maybe someday I'll be able to give someone else a word of encouragement."

As they drove into the driveway, Todd's vintage car was there. Todd was in the house playing a game of dominoes with Ben.

"You're back!" Ben jumped up, scattering the dominoes. He ran across the room to embrace his mother. "Dad said I could stay up so you could tuck me in."

Mrs. Leighton and Benjamin disappeared up the stairs.

Todd smiled at Lexi. "How did it go?"

Lexi sank into the chair across from him. "Fine, great, terrific . . . awful."

"But you were smiling when you came inside. I thought everything must have been great."

"Actually it was. The people were very nice. Everyone was outgoing and hopeful."

"Then what's the problem?"

"I'm encouraged for a while. Then this anger comes bubbling up from inside me and I don't know where it comes from or what to do about it. Why did this have to happen to my mom? She's never done anything wrong to anyone. Why her?" Tears welled in Lexi's eyes.

She was about to wipe them away when Todd reached for her hands and drew them back to her lap. "Cry, Lexi, let it out."

"But it's so stupid and I feel so selfish!"

"Cry. Get angry. It's all right. You have a right to be angry too." Todd's compassionate understanding was the straw that broke the camel's back. The tears that Lexi had been holding back for so long flooded from her. Tenderly Todd gathered her into his arms and held her, rocking her back and forth as if she were a tiny child. "It's okay, Lexi. It's okay to cry."

Lexi didn't know how long she wept, but as quickly as the tears came, they seemed to disappear. She hiccuped and gave Todd a teary, bleary-eyed smile. "Sorry about that."

He touched her hair and smiled at her. "Don't be sorry. I like the way you look with a red nose and puffy eyes."

"Right." Lexi smiled again in spite of herself. "Tonight I finally understood how my mom felt when she first learned she had MS. I felt so angry. The anger was just boiling inside me not doing any good, only harm."

"Now?" Todd wondered.

"Some of it's gone. It disappeared with my tears." Lexi gave Todd a hug. "I needed to let it all out, I guess. Thanks for being here for me."

"Anytime. You know that." They sat together in the chair, Lexi snuggled into the crook of Todd's arm, her head resting on his shoulder.

"Mom's right," Lexi finally spoke. "It is time to

start living again. I've been moaning and groaning around here for too long. The MS is going to be with us from now on, but we don't have to give it every minute of every day."

"Good, Lexi. I'm glad you've realized that." Todd put his arms around her and held her tightly.

# Chapter Eight

"I can't make it. Go ahead. Save yourself. Don't wait for me."

"Come on, Binky. This was your idea."

"My legs have quit working. I can't breathe. I'm going to faint. Go ahead without me, Lexi. Just send Egg back to pick me up."

"If you're going to wait for your brother to pick you up, you'll be lying on the sidewalk a long time. Keep running, Binky. This was your plan."

"It was a stupid idea. What made me think that jogging is good for you? I think it's going to kill me." Binky's face was red with exertion. Sweat dropped off the end of her nose. "I never knew running was so hard."

"We probably shouldn't have gone an entire mile the first time out. You set your goal a little high."

"*You're* not exhausted," Binky complained. Her "run" slowed to a crawl.

"That's because I'm in better shape than you are."

"It's not fair. This is *my* self-improvement program. You should be as much of a mess as I am."

"Your idea of exercise has always been carrying

a bowl of popcorn from the kitchen to the living room."

"And I'm paying for it now. I'm going to have cramps in my legs tonight."

"I think I must have cramps in my head for doing this with you," Lexi said with a laugh. "Come on. We're only a block from my house."

Binky dug deep and found a burst of energy which carried her up the Leightons' sidewalk and through their kitchen door.

"Hello, girls. I've been waiting for you." Mrs. Leighton was in the kitchen holding a large perspiring pitcher of lemonade. "Thirsty?"

"I could drink an ocean." Binky collapsed into one of the kitchen chairs.

"How about a glass of freshly made lemonade instead?"

Binky took a glass in both hands and drank deeply.

Lexi took the glass her mother handed her and sat down across from Binky. "Join us, Mom?"

"I'd love too. I want to visit with you for a few minutes."

"You want to talk to *us*?" Binky looked surprised. "Adults never want to talk to me."

"I wanted to tell you girls how proud I am of what you're doing for yourselves. I think Binky's self-improvement plan is a wonderful idea. I'm glad you're taking part in it, Lexi."

"You are?" Binky and Lexi chimed together.

"Yes, I am. I see now how important it is to take care of yourself and not to take your health for granted. I've always been an advocate of a healthy lifestyle, but now with my illness I realize just how important it is."

"It's nice of you to say that, Mrs. Leighton," Binky said. "At my house, everyone thinks I'm nuts."

"Maybe that's because you're trying to get them to go on your self-improvement plan too, Binky," Lexi chided gently.

"They need it worse than I do, whether they realize it or not," Binky said self-righteously.

"They just haven't had a wake-up call about their health yet, Binky," Mrs. Leighton said with a smile. "I know I certainly got mine. Now I'm eager to learn everything I can about taking care of myself."

"What are you doing, Mrs. Leighton?" Binky asked, ever curious.

"I learn something new every day. Temperature can aggravate MS. I may be affected if I spend too much time in the sun at the beach, sit too long in a very hot bathtub, or run a fever."

"Weird," Binky said.

"My new friend, Mrs. Janzen, says that it's wise for MS patients to avoid too much sunbathing or hot tubs or showers or being out during the warmest part of the summer day. Cold weather can be just as debilitating so I'll have to work hard to keep the temperature inside my body and outside my body on an even keel. It is important for patients with MS to monitor their physical exertion and not to get too tired. Fatigue can lead to an MS attack. People in my support group say that it's dangerous to work too much *or* play too much."

"I didn't think you could play too much," Binky

said. "What do you do if that happens?"

"Go to bed and rest up. Often rest is enough to make the symptoms pass. I also need to take care of myself during the flu season because colds and flu can start MS attacks."

"You aren't talking about self-improvement, Mrs. Leighton," Binky said. "You're talking about *survival.*"

Mrs. Leighton laughed out loud. "I guess you could say that, but I'd rather think of it as self-improvement, or at least self-help."

Binky studied Mrs. Leighton with serious eyes. "I think you're very brave."

Unexpectedly, Binky threw her arms around the older woman. "I'd like to be just like you."

Mrs. Leighton hugged Binky tightly. "What a beautiful thing to say."

"Lexi's really lucky she has you for a mom."

"Oh, Binky," Mrs. Leighton gathered both the girls close to her for another hug. She wiped a piece of damp hair out of Binky's eyes. "And I'd like to have a daughter just like you—if I could pick a sister for Lexi, that is.

"Don't get so involved with your self-improvement program that you forget it's supposed to be fun. The reason you're doing it is for *you*, not to impress anyone else. Do it because you know it's the best thing for Binky McNaughton, okay?"

"You know me awfully well, don't you, Mrs. Leighton?"

"Binky, I can read you like a book." Mrs. Leighton laughed.

"At first I *was* on this self-improvement kick for all the wrong reasons. I wanted to do it to keep

Harry's interest. I saw all those beautiful girls at his college and I thought that if I didn't make changes in myself, he'd lose interest in me. But that's not the reason I'm continuing to make changes in my life. Now I'm doing it for me. If Harry likes me better this way, great. If he doesn't, too bad."

"That's the spirit, Binky," Mrs. Leighton said. She poured a third glass of lemonade and sat down at the table with the girls. "Tell me about your run. . . ."

---

"Where are you going?" Lexi met her mother at the front door. Mrs. Leighton was in jeans, a white T-shirt, and a colorful blazer. She had had her hair done and was wearing a new pair of sunglasses. "I'm going shopping with two ladies I met at my support group, Connie Janzen and Janet Schuler."

"Shopping? It's been *ages* since I've been to the mall."

"You've been to the mall three or four times in the last week!"

"I know, but just to walk around, not to do any *real* shopping."

"Is there something you need?"

Lexi looked down at her feet. "New tennis shoes."

"Are you hinting that you'd like to come along?"

"Could I?"

"Long enough to pick out new shoes."

"And then I'll leave you alone. I promise."

"You don't have to promise that. I'd love to have Connie and Janet meet you. Grab your jacket."

They met Mrs. Leighton's friends at the Food Court. Connie Janzen was tall and attractive. Lexi remembered her from the meeting at the hospital. Janet Schuler was blond, round-faced, and used a wheelchair.

"I brought my daughter along," Mrs. Leighton explained. "She wanted a new pair of tennis shoes."

"We can cover a lot of territory today. I can see that already. There's nothing I like better than a serious day of shopping. How about you?" Janet turned to Lexi with a twinkle in her eye.

"Maybe I do need a few things other than tennis shoes," Lexi said slyly. "I can get an outfit or two for school and some new jeans and—"

"I didn't invite you along to put me into bankruptcy, Lexi," her mother said with a laugh. "Shoes and jeans, that's all you need today."

The afternoon flew by. Marilyn Leighton was as lighthearted and cheerful as Lexi had seen her in a long time, thanks to Connie Janzen and Janet Schuler, but always ready with a witty or sarcastic remark anytime the subject of multiple sclerosis came up. When Marilyn and Connie wandered into a shoe department, Lexi stayed behind with Janet who was busy sampling perfume testers.

"Mrs. Schuler," she began.

"Please call me Janet. We're shopping buddies. The best kind of friends."

"I was wondering," Lexi stammered, "how do you do it?"

"Do what?"

"Stay so cheerful. You know, in your wheelchair and all? Isn't it terribly hard? Aren't you afraid sometimes?"

Janet spritzed a dab of perfume on the back of her wrist and inhaled deeply. She set the atomizer back on the counter before turning to Lexi.

"Sure I get frightened and frustrated. I wouldn't be human if I didn't. Even shopping, much as I love it, can be difficult—especially when I'm having trouble with my eyes. I used to with friends that didn't have MS, but I found out that it's easier to shop with someone who understands. Sometimes I feel weak and need to go home. It's hard to explain that to someone who still has things to do. That's why I enjoy coming with Connie and your mom. They understand my pace and I understand theirs."

"Don't you feel left out sometimes?"

"Left out? Oh no. I'm very busy. This," Janet patted the arm of the wheelchair, "doesn't hold me back at all. I teach Sunday school and work at a part-time job. My husband is a wonderful cook and I'm great at giving directions, so we do a lot of entertaining. I live my life to the fullest. I've always been that way and I'm certainly not going to let MS prevent me from enjoying life. I refuse to curl up and die."

Lexi studied Janet's round brown face, so sincere and compelling. "Then you really are just the same person you were before you were diagnosed with MS. Changing your lifestyle didn't mean you changed who you are."

Janet's expression softened. "That's how it will be for your mom too, Lexi. She's still the same person she was before this illness."

The warm sense of comfort and relief ran through Lexi. Her mom was still her same old mom. That was the most important thing of all.

# Chapter Nine

*"She's still mom, she's still mom. Things will get better. She's still mom."* It was a chant Lexi ran over and over in her mind. Every time some new symptom cropped up, or a new wave of depression blindsided Mrs. Leighton, Lexi repeated the litany. Every day had new challenges, new hurdles to cross.

"I'm sorry, Lexi, I didn't mean to stumble like that."

"You couldn't help it, mom." Lexi helped her mom to the sofa and wrapped a blanket around her waist. "Just rest for a little while and you'll feel better."

"The doctor warned us that MS was a disease the entire family would suffer," Mrs. Leighton said. "I never realized how true or painful that statement was at the time." She punched a curled fist into one of the soft pillows of the couch.

"I get so frustrated. One day I feel fine and the next it's as though everything has fallen apart for me. "I can't take much more of this roller coaster ride."

"Why don't you get out of the house for a while? Go to the art store. Spend as much time there as you want. I'll take care of Ben."

Mrs. Leighton shook her head dispiritedly. "I can't, Lexi. There's no way I can drive to the store. I might have an accident and hurt someone. I couldn't live with that."

"Just because you had a little fender bender in the parking lot at the mall doesn't mean you can't drive. Dad's always said parking lots are dangerous places to drive. The lady who hit you backed right out into you."

"My reaction time was slowed. I couldn't get to the brake in time."

"But it wasn't your fault."

"I feel too unsafe to drive, Lexi. That's all there is to it."

"Even the police officer who investigated the accident said it wasn't your fault!"

"He couldn't know how heavy and slow my leg felt as I was trying to lift it from the accelerator to the brake. Perhaps the other woman *did* cause the accident, but I could have prevented it if my body had been functioning properly. I can't trust myself. I can't even make a decent breakfast anymore. Why would I think I could drive a vehicle? I could kill someone."

Mrs. Leighton referred to the breakfast fiasco that morning. She was carrying a gallon of milk from the refrigerator to the table when her fingers refused to hold it any longer. It dropped to the floor sending splashed milk all around the kitchen. It had taken Lexi, Dr. Leighton, and Benjamin almost half an hour to clean up the mess. Just when they'd sat down again to eat, Mrs. Leighton had dropped

Benjamin's pancakes on the floor. It had not been a good morning.

Mrs. Leighton sat on the couch staring out the window. People were outside moving around, cleaning up their yards, fixing their cars. "It's so hard not to be jealous of them, Lexi."

"You've never fixed a car in your life. Why would you want to start now?"

"It's not wanting to, Lexi. It's the idea of knowing you can't."

Lexi was relieved to hear the telephone ring. She had no idea what to do when her mother was in a state like this.

"I'd like to speak to Lexi Leighton please."

"Speaking."

"Hi, Lexi. My name is April Janzen. You don't know me, but . . ."

"Janzen, as in Connie Janzen?"

"That's right. She's my mom. She said I should call you. She thought it might help you to talk to another teenager who's gone through what you're experiencing right now. My mom's had MS for years. I've had a lot of experience with MS from a daughter's point of view. Do you want to talk?"

Lexi grabbed on to the offer like a drowning person might clutch for a lifeline. "Yes. Any time you're free."

"How about this afternoon? I don't have anything special planned."

"This afternoon would be fine. I've been needing someone to talk to," Lexi said softly so that her mother couldn't hear.

"I know how it goes," April said sympathetically. "Hang in there. Let's meet at the Mexican place east of the mall. They have great nachos and don't mind if you sit there all afternoon when they aren't busy."

"Sounds fine to me," Lexi said.

"See you in an hour?"

"I'll be there."

Lexi hung up the phone feeling both relief and excitement. April Janzen sounded normal and happy. Maybe there was a chance that someday Lexi could feel that way too.

---

Lexi knew immediately that it was April standing at the entrance, beneath a huge garishly decorated sombrero. April reminded Lexi of her mother, Connie.

April's narrow face broke into a wide grin. "Hi, I'm April." She gestured at the tacky sombreros and gaily colored shawls decorating the entry. "I hope this is all right with you," she said. Music, heavy on castanets, played in the background. "I find this place cheerful, for some reason. Maybe it's all the bright colors or the music. Besides they have the world's best salsa here. I've already got a table."

Lexi followed April into the main room to a small table in one corner. "I thought this would be private. Is that all right?"

Lexi nodded mutely. April had thought of everything. Lexi's concerns about feeling uncomfortable vanished.

April sat down with a dramatic flair. She had a surprising presence for a teenager—confident, calm, capable. She also had the reddest hair and bluest eyes Lexi had ever seen. April was taller and thinner than Lexi had expected she might be. She also smiled a lot. "Do you like it?" April slipped her hair behind her ear and tugged on her earlobe.

"Like what?" Lexi said, staring at the jeweled ear.

"I just got a third hole. Neat, huh? Mom thinks I'm crazy, but she said as long as I spent my own money, she wouldn't say anything. No more, though."

The waitress came by with salsa and chips. "Are you ready to order?" she asked.

April looked over at Lexi. "Do you mind if we have the seafood nachos? They're stupendous."

"Fine with me," Lexi said, willing to be swept along in April's confident wake.

"One order of nachos and then later an order of sopapillas with honey and chocolate sauce. Two large lemonades to drink." She turned to Lexi. "Is that all right?"

After the waitress had disappeared, Lexi grinned. "You must come here often."

"Yes, and I always order the same thing. Sorry if I seem bossy. I just know what's good. My mother says if I were born a machine, I'd be a bulldozer. I plow my way into and out of things sometimes. You aren't used to me. I apologize. I'll try to slow down."

"That's all right." Lexi liked April more and more. "It's nice to have someone think for me. My brain's just about worn out."

April leaned back in her chair, crossed her arms over her chest, and studied Lexi compassionately. "It's been tough, huh?"

Much to Lexi's dismay, tears suddenly filled her eyes. She wiped them away, but not so quickly that

April didn't see them. "Yes, it has."

"Bummer. I know how it goes."

April's sympathy meant much more to Lexi than that of any of her friends. It wasn't that Peggy, Binky, or Jennifer were unkind or unsympathetic, but it was just that April had been there. She knew how it was. Her mother had MS too. Somehow April's compassion was almost too much for Lexi to bear.

"It's okay if you want to cry, you know," April said bluntly. "When my mom was first diagnosed, I didn't think it was okay to cry either. I was wrong. It's scary—really scary. You don't know what's going to happen to your mom. You wonder if she's going to change or if your life will change. When Mom got sick, it was one of the very worst times in my own life. Crummier yet was that I felt guilty about feeling selfish and worrying about myself when my mom was having such a hard time. Guilt is good for nothing, but it seems to be everywhere."

"I feel all of that and more," Lexi admitted. "Our family is on this huge emotional roller coaster ride and we can't get off, any of us. The only one who's taking it pretty well is my little brother Ben. He has Down's syndrome. Everybody's been trying to protect him from what's been going on."

"Maybe there's nothing to protect him from," April suggested.

Lexi looked at her in surprise. "What do you mean?"

"Maybe your mom will do really well," she suggested.

"What if she doesn't? What if she ends up in a wheelchair?"

"Then she'll end up in a wheelchair," April said. "But it's not going to help to worry about it in advance, is it?"

"No, I suppose not."

"Then don't. It's wasted energy. Trust me on this one. I worried for two years that my mom was going to be bedridden or using canes or a wheelchair. Then I realized I was wasting time worrying about something I couldn't do anything about. That's one thing MS does. It teaches you to live for the day, not for the future. We have a celebration every day that my mom feels good. You know what? We've had a lot of celebrations."

"How's it been for your mom?" Lexi wondered. She'd never dared to ask what it really was going to be like living with someone with MS. She sensed April would tell her the truth.

"It's been pretty typical. She's had several attacks with recoveries following. She's been lucky enough not to suffer any permanent damage. She has very few restrictions in her life. She holds down a job and takes care of our family. Most of the time we forget she is ill at all. Our good friend, Janice, has been different. She's slowly gotten worse. Mom's doctor told her that three quarters of all MS patients will never need a wheelchair and despite everything else it does to a person, it rarely causes a death."

"That's a relief!" Lexi said.

"I remember when it first started for us. My mom complained of numbness and tingling in her leg. It lasted about six or eight weeks and then disappeared. The next time we heard anything about her health, she said her vision was blurring. She went to the eye doctor for new glasses, but he couldn't seem to get the right prescription. She still has trouble with her eyes sometimes. Then she started to complain about numbness, double vision, or weird burning sensations. We told her to go to the doctor. That's when she was diagnosed. Flare-ups and remissions are all pretty regular. Now when we see Mom walking into the kitchen dragging one leg, we say, 'Oh, oh, there she goes again.' "

"You can *laugh* about this?" Lexi said in amazement.

"Laugh or cry," April said with a shrug. "Might as well laugh. Mom laughs too. She's been great. It took her awhile to accept things, but since she started working with the support group, she's gotten stronger and stronger."

The waitress arrived with the seafood nachos. April began eating enthusiastically. Lexi, who hadn't felt hungry, decided the nachos looked pretty good after all. April's no-nonsense, matter-of-fact discussion of MS was a great relief to her.

Gathering her courage, she ventured to admit something she'd been keeping buried deep inside. "It's hard, sometimes, not to be mad at Mom. It doesn't seem fair, but I can't help it. Sometimes I just want to yell, 'Why did you *do* this to me? to our family?' "

Waiting for April's shock and disapproval, Lexi was surprised to see the girl nod knowingly. "I know. I was really bummed with my mom too. Somehow I thought she should *stop* this. I felt like it was a dirty trick to be playing on me. Pretty selfish, I know, but normal. We talked to a counselor about it. Don't worry about it. Those feelings will go away."

"They will?" Suddenly Lexi was feeling much better. Even her appetite was coming back.

"What if your mother starts getting worse and doesn't improve again?" Lexi wondered.

"We'll deal with it. What other choice do we have? We built a new house two years ago. Dad made sure the whole thing was wheelchair accessible. We put heat in our front sidewalk so that ice never forms there. He didn't want Mom or any of her friends to slip and fall on an icy patch. We have an attached garage so Mom doesn't have to step on snow and ice when she gets out of the car. The bathtub has handrails in it so she doesn't slip and fall. Those are all improvements that every house should have. *That*'s how we're dealing with it—by trying to be realistic rather than afraid. Also, my mom has been very up-front with her friends and family. When she gets frightened or depressed, she knows who to call."

"You make it sound so easy. . . ."

"When she was first diagnosed she didn't dare tell her boss that she had MS. Instead she told him she'd hurt her knee or twisted her ankle. When she finally got up the nerve to go to her boss and tell him what her *real* problem was, she discovered he was genuinely sympathetic and wanted to be helpful. He asked her to be in charge of watching out for things around the office that would make it difficult for someone with a disability."

"You make it sound as though MS is no problem at all for your family."

"Do I? I don't mean to. It's been a bad problem

for us, but we're coping. *That*'s what I'm trying to tell you. When I found out that mom had MS, I wish I'd had someone sit down with me and say, 'Hey, you're going to make it. You're going to be all right. This isn't the end of the world. It feels like it right now, but it really isn't.' *That*'s what I'm trying to tell you. You might not believe it from other people, but *I've* been there."

Lexi realized with a start that she and April had finished thc nachos. The waitress was replacing the empty plates with a platter of sopapillas.

"I can't tell you exactly how it will be for you," April admitted, "but just keeping things in perspective helps. When Mom is exhausted and aching all over, I offer to run a warm bath for her. I always use lots of bubbles and get the bathroom ready for her. I turn the lights off, have candles burning and music playing. I help her climb into the tub and put a little plastic blow-up pillow behind her head. While she's soaking, I'll make supper. She says that's the best medicine she's found for MS." April grinned.

"Sometimes, when I see that she's aching, I give her a back massage and offer to finish something she's started. When her eyes are giving her trouble, I'll read to her. We also get audio books so that Mom can keep up with all the latest bestsellers without having to strain her eyes." April shrugged nonchalantly. "It doesn't sound like much, but every little bit helps. You just learn to cope, Lexi. Things are different, but they aren't always awful."

"It's a little bit like Ben, then."

April appeared puzzled.

"He's not 'normal' like other kids. We always

have to make accommodations for him. He goes to the Academy for the Handicapped. He doesn't catch on to things as quickly as others his age. His coordination isn't very good, but our family has learned to adapt. We give Ben a little more time and are sure not to rush him because that makes him even more clumsy."

"It's sort of the same way with MS patients," April admitted.

"But having Ben around is worth the extra trouble," Lexi continued. "He's so cheerful, funny, loving, and sweet that it doesn't seem to matter that it takes him twice as long to tie his shoes or that we have to keep going over and over what he learns so he doesn't forget it. We make accommodations for him and try to make things easier for him, but—" Lexi paused to consider. "But, it isn't a hardship for us. We've just made all those things a part of our lives."

"Exactly," April crowed. "And that's what you'll do for your mom, too. It just seems weird and foreign right now, but it won't after a while. Don't get me wrong—it's *not* always easy. Sometimes it's miserable."

"My mom told me that your family are Christians," Lexi said. "We are too."

"That's great! When you've tried everything and it's failed, at least you know that you have another source to tap into for some help. 'Come to me, all you who are weary and burdened, and I will give you rest.' That's one that's helped our family a lot."

Lexi glanced at her watch. "Do you realize we've been here almost three hours? My parents are going to worry!"

"No problem. Your mom will call mine. My mother will tell her I'm a chatterbox and that you're fine."

"Thank you, April. This is one of the nicest things anyone has ever done for me."

"It was easy. Besides, I'd like to get to know you better, Lexi."

"I'd like that too."

"Call anytime."

As Lexi drove toward home, she felt more carefree than she had in days. She no longer felt so alone or that she was carrying the weight of her mother's illness on her own shoulders.

April had said some pretty wise things that Lexi was determined to remember. What's more, there was an extra bonus. She really liked April. She had a hunch they could become good friends, given the opportunity.

She pulled into the garage and turned off the ignition. She punched the button on the automatic garage door opener and watched it close in the rearview mirror. She pounded gently on the steering wheel, a little gesture of anticipation and excitement. She was feeling better than she had in a long, long time.

# Chapter Ten

"Wake up, sleepyhead. It's a beautiful day. You're going to miss it lazing in bed."

Lexi opened one eye. Her mother was bustling through the bedroom, pulling up shades and picking up crumpled clothing. "It's Saturday morning. I'm sleeping in."

"Nonsense. You're coming with me. We're going for a drive."

"We are?" Lexi rolled over to stare at her mother. Mrs. Leighton was dressed in trim navy slacks and a white blouse. Her hair was styled and she was wearing makeup. She looked wonderful. "Where are we going?"

"There's an art show in Milltown that I want to see. I thought it would be fun if we made a day of it. We can drive over to the show, have lunch, do a little shopping, and come home. Sound good to you?"

Lexi nodded dumbly, unable to speak. A change had come over her mother in the past few days. It was as though the bleak, dark days when Mrs. Leighton had learned she had MS had vanished. This was her mother as she *used* to be—cheerful, chipper, energetic, enthusiastic.

"What's going on?" Lexi rolled to the side of the bed and sat up.

"Going on? I just told you. We'll go to the art show, then have lunch—"

"Not about that. I mean what's going on with you? You seem more . . ."

" . . . normal," Mrs. Leighton finished for her daughter.

"I wasn't going to say that."

"But that's what you were thinking, wasn't it?"

Lexi hung her head sheepishly.

"All right, I haven't been normal for quite some time, but I'm working on it."

"What's made the difference, Mom?"

Mrs. Leighton sat down on the bed beside Lexi. "The MS support group has helped me a great deal. I've been talking to Pastor Lake. He's given me lots of insight about myself and about the ways that I should manage my illness. Both helped me to make some decisions."

"What sort of decisions?"

"I'm not going to let my MS hold me back," Mrs. Leighton said firmly. "I've said all this before but this time I really *mean* it. I'm feeling better. Maybe, according to my doctor, I could be one of the lucky ones with very few flare-ups or even symptoms. It's an unpredictable disease. I think I should hope for the best, even while I'm preparing for the worst. That means I'm not going to waste my good days by moping around the house, worrying about what might be coming down the road. Instead of stewing about the bad days, which may or may not come, I'm going to celebrate every minute that I feel good." At that moment the doorbell rang.

It was so good to hear her mother talk like this, Lexi hated to have her interrupted. She got up to see who was at the front door.

"I decided to see how your family is doing," Jennifer said. Her expression and words were pointed. Everyone knew it hadn't been good at the Leighton household for some time.

"Better. Much better."

"You mean it?" Jennifer asked as Mrs. Leighton walked into the entry.

"You look great!" Jennifer blurted. "I mean, you always look great, but you look especially great today."

Mrs. Leighton laughed. "I know exactly what you mean, Jennifer. I feel great too. I really do. Not only physically, but mentally."

"What happened?" Always blunt and to the point, Jennifer made both Lexi and her mother smile.

"I got tired of moping around the house. The pity party is over."

"How does a person do that?" Jennifer wondered.

"By refusing to attend the party any longer," Mrs. Leighton said with a chuckle. "And deciding not to focus on the disease all the time, but to focus on life instead. That MS is going to be a problem . . . there's no doubt about it, but I can't let it ruin every single part of my life.

"Come into the kitchen," she invited. "Warm caramel rolls on the counter."

"You can smell food a mile away," Lexi accused as Jennifer followed her into the kitchen.

Mrs. Leighton served up a roll for each of the girls.

"I can't believe the difference in you," Jennifer said honestly.

"I do feel younger and more energetic. And a whole lot wiser too." Mrs. Leighton poured herself a cup of coffee and sat down on a stool across from Lexi and Jennifer.

"I'm smarter too. I now know what Psalms 55:22 means. 'Cast your cares on the LORD and he will sustain you; he will never let the righteous fall.' He's helped me a lot in the past few weeks. I don't know what I would have done if I hadn't had Him to turn to for strength."

"Awesome," Jennifer enthused.

"He really is," Mrs. Leighton said with a smile. "I've also made some wonderful new friends through my group," Mrs. Leighton continued. "They've helped me to see that I should continue painting even though it might be more difficult for me than it has been in the past. Lexi's dad and I have already talked about making the studio wheelchair accessible—just in case."

"You didn't tell me that, Mom," Lexi looked alarmed.

"Don't be so worried," Mrs. Leighton said lightly. "I'm not planning to use that wheelchair access, but if I have to, then at least I'll be able to get into the studio to paint. That will cheer me immensely. You know that. Now instead of standing to paint, I'm going to adjust my easel so I can use a stool or a chair. It's the same as resting before I get tired, Lexi. Watchfulness and preparation are entirely different behaviors than submission and defeat. I'm *not* going to let this disease get to me. It might change my life, but it can't destroy it."

"You're really incredible, Mrs. Leighton," Jennifer said. "I remember how rotten I felt before I was diagnosed as having dyslexia. I thought I was the most stupid, unappealing person in the whole world. You've got a condition much worse than dyslexia and you're being really brave."

"But you struggle with your dyslexia every day, don't you?"

"I listen to tapes instead of reading books and my mom helps me with homework."

"That's what I mean. Do what you have to do and then forget about it. Jennifer, everyone has something in their life that's a little harder for them than it is for other people. We're not perfect. We must do the best we can. Sometimes even something wonderful comes of what is negative."

"What wonderful thing can come from MS?" Lexi said doubtfully.

Mrs. Leighton grinned broadly. "There's something I haven't told you, something I've been thinking about for the past few weeks. Your father and I have been discussing it and I've decided that I'm going to do it."

"What? What? What?" Jennifer chirped. "What are you going to do?"

"I'm going to write a book."

Lexi and Jennifer stared at Mrs. Leighton in mute amazement. "A book? About what?"

"I'm going to write a book for children who have a parent with MS or any another serious illness. I want the book to help children understand what their mom or dad might be going through. After I was diagnosed, I went to the library looking for just such a book for you or for Ben. There was nothing on the shelves that would help me. It would have been easier for Ben if I'd had such a book. I'm going to illustrate it myself. Frankly, I'm more excited about this than anything I've done in a long, long time. It's a way I can combine my love of art and children into one creation."

"Mom, I think that's a fabulous idea." Lexi jumped up from her chair and moved around the counter to hug her mother. "I would have loved a book like that. It would have made it so much easier for all of us."

"Maybe I can turn this disease into something really good for myself and for others." Mrs. Leighton's eyes were shining. "Who knows? The best contributions of my life might be as a result of this illness."

"Wow! I'm going to know a real author. Can I have your autograph?" Jennifer urged.

"As many times as you want."

"When are you going to start writing?"

"I've already made some notes and done some preliminary sketches."

"A book!" Lexi sat back and crossed her arms over her chest. "Great idea."

Mrs. Leighton was thoughtful. When she spoke, her voice was dreamy and faraway. "Until now, I never knew what to think of the old cliche, 'When God shuts a door, He opens a window,' but I really do sense a 'window' opening here for me. My life has changed in many ways, but perhaps it will be richer, more meaningful, and more creative than I'd ever dreamed possible."

"This is really neat." Jennifer's eyes were shining. "You're an inspiration, Mrs. Leighton, and I'm sure your book is going to be a great success. You're going to be famous."

They were all laughing when the doorbell rang. It was Binky.

"Oh hi, Bink, come on in. . . ." Lexi paused. She stared hard at her friend as though seeing her for the very first time. Binky had changed. She'd gotten a new haircut, which was very flattering to her small features. Her hair was shiny and bouncy. Her skin was clear. Binky even looked as though she'd built a few small muscles. Her stance was square and straight. She looked very . . . healthy.

"Binky, you look wonderful. What have you done to yourself?"

A grin spread across Binky's features. "Do you really mean it? You notice a difference?"

"I do. I haven't seen you for a few days and just now, when you were standing there, you looked so . . . so different. I think your self-improvement plan has really paid off."

Binky looked like a kitten who'd just eaten a bowl of cream. "That's the nicest thing anyone's said to me in weeks!" she crowed. "Except, of course, for what Harry said on the phone last night . . . ."

"Harry called?"

"What did he say?"

"Just that I was still the most special girl in the whole world." Binky's eyes gleamed. "And that he couldn't wait to come home and see me. Apparently Todd and Egg told him I'd been lifting weights and that I was looking good."

"*Egg* said that?"

"I know. I could hardly believe it myself. Apparently my brother isn't brain dead after all." Binky glowed. "But the best part was this: Harry told me that he didn't even care what I looked like on the outside because I was such a neat person on the inside! He said that any improvements I made were just going to be 'frosting on the cake'!"

"You've got yourself a winner, Binky!" Lexi said.

Binky looked fondly at the girls as they stood facing her. "I'm no dummy. I've surrounded myself with winners—like you guys, for instance."

"Group hug!" Jennifer squealed as the three of them dissolved into laughter.

Just then, Lexi noticed her mother standing in the kitchen doorway, watching and smiling.

*Winners*. They were all going to be winners. She was sure of it.

When Egg and Binky are appointed managers of the student-run Cedar River School store, no one is certain what will happen next. Will their innovative ideas bring them A's in marketing class or destroy the small business entirely? Unless they discover who is stealing cash from the store and put a stop to it, all will be ruined. And do they really *want* to catch the thief—especially if their suspicions are confirmed and it is a friend who is guilty of the deed? Discover the answer in Cedar River Daydreams #24

# A Note From Judy

I'm glad you're reading *Cedar River Daydreams*! I hope I've given you something to think about as well as a story to entertain you. If you feel you have any of the problems that Lexi and her friends experience, I encourage you to talk with your parents, a pastor, or a trusted adult friend. There are many people who care about you!

I love to hear from my readers, so if you'd like to receive my newsletter and a bookmark, please send a self-addressed, stamped envelope to:

Judy Baer
Bethany House Publishers
11300 Hampshire Avenue South
Minneapolis, MN 55438

---

Be sure to watch for my newest *Dear Judy . . .* books at your local bookstore. These books are full of questions that you, my readers, have asked in your letters, along with my response. Just about every topic is covered—from dating and romance to friendships and parents. Hope to hear from you soon!

*Dear Judy, What's It Like at Your House?*
*Dear Judy, Did You Ever Like a Boy*

Turn the page for an exciting
Sneak Preview
of

*Sarah's Dilemma*,

Book #4 in the
LIVE! FROM BRENTWOOD HIGH series
by Judy Baer

# Sarah's Dilemma

JUDY BAER

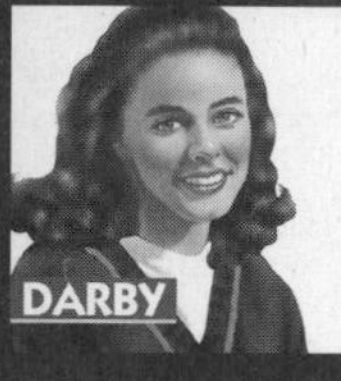


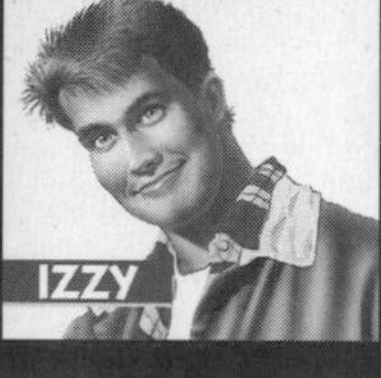

"Look out! Coming through!" The honking sound of a cheap toy horn challenged the noise of Chaos Central. "Out of my way!" Everyone in the media room turned to see who—or what—was coming through the door.

Sarah Riley rolled into the room with a theatrical flair, squeezing an orange rubber globe attached to the little black horn that was making such a racket. Her red hair looked windblown, as though she'd put her wheelchair into warp speed down the halls of Brentwood High. The vehicle in question was decorated with foil-covered blazes of mock lightning.

"Am I late?"

"For the moon shot? Yes. The rocket left fifteen minutes ago. Of course, I suppose you could blast off in that thing." Izzy Mooney sauntered over to Sarah, a half-eaten candy bar in his hand. "What's with the horn?"

"I was late for class twice yesterday. Too much congestion in the halls. I decided that if I didn't want any more tardy slips, I would have to take matters into my own hands." Sarah honked the tinny-sounding horn. "What do you think?"

"I know *I'd* get out of your way," Jake Saunders said, dimples flashing deep in his cheeks.

"Good. Then it works." Sarah relaxed against the back of her chair. She was dressed in a bright orange jacket and equally vibrant yellow turtleneck above her blue jeans. Her socks matched her outfit—one was yellow, the other orange. The vivid colors highlighted the warm red of her hair and the pale ivory of her skin. Sarah looked as cheerful as she sounded.

"Hi, Julie. What's happening? Molly, I love your outfit! Josh, new haircut?" She wheeled her way around the room greeting the student staff of *Live! From Brentwood High.*

Her characteristic good humor was met with something less than warmth.

"Who put a quarter in you, Riley? Hasn't anyone told you it's morning?" Kate Akima's dark eyes glittered unpleasantly. "I don't like when people are too cheerful before noon."

"I think she put too much sugar on her cereal. She's on a high," Andrew Tremaine concluded. "She'll get over it."

"What's with you people today?" Sarah asked, unoffended by the response of her friends and co-workers. This crew worked together for the student-run television station at Brentwood High. They'd all seen each other in far worse moods than this.

"I wish you wouldn't be so cheerful all the time," Molly muttered. "You put the rest of us to shame. I was just complaining about what an awful day it is and then you roll in acting like it's the best day of the year!"

Julie Osborn, whom Izzy had once deemed the "Official Pain in the Neck" of the media room, scowled at Sarah. "Some days you're so sweet you give me cavities, Riley. Today's one of those days." Julie paused to consider. "It's that Christian stuff with you, isn't it?"

Sarah burst out laughing. The only admitted Christian on the television staff, she was an oddity to most of the students. Every time Sarah did something unexpected, her friends blamed it on the fact that either (a) she was a Christian, or (b) she used a wheelchair.

"Actually, it's more the fact that I'm a morning person, Julie. My mom's a Christian, but even she can't smile until she's had her morning coffee."

"Then I like your mother. Anyone who's grumpy in the morning can't be all bad."

"Ignore them," Darby Ellison advised as she walked toward Sarah. "There must be a change in the weather. Everybody is crabby today."

"She'll be crabby too once she hears what Ms. Wright has planned for us," Kate warned dourly. "Just wait."

"So what's the bad news? Are we covering toxic waste?"

"Worse. She says we have to start doing reviews—both for the television show and for the newspaper." In addition to the weekly *Live! From Brentwood High* student-run cable television show, the production class also put out a small paper and had an occasional radio show. None of the students were as enthused about these projects as they were about the TV show. There was always much griping and complaining when assignments were being made.

"What kind of reviews? Books? Movies?"

"Now the news gets *really* horrible. We have to review a *play*."

"What's so bad about that? I love plays."

"You would," Julie grumbled. "There's a new production opening at that little old theater downtown. You know the one, it looks like Shakespeare used it for his own plays—when he was still alive."

"I can't believe Ms. Wright would make us go to that mousetrap and sit through some boring garbage! There are three new movies opening at the Cineplex and we're stuck going to the theater." Andrew looked disgusted, as if someone had made a royal infringement on his time.

"Well, I think it sounds like fun!" Sarah said. "What about you, Darby?"

"It's fine with me. I don't have an allergy to culture like these illiterates do."

"Call me whatever you want," Julie said haughtily. "Just don't make me go."

"We have ten tickets," Darby explained. "Ms. Wright wants us to use them all. We're supposed to work in teams of two on the reviews. A 'thumbs up, thumbs down' sort of thing. Four will do the package for the TV show, the rest will do a column for the paper."

"Who's going?"

"So far, no one. We need volunteers."

"Count me out," Kate chimed. "I wouldn't go into that old rat-infested theater for anything."

"It's being renovated."

"That probably means they boarded the rats into the walls."

"Gross! I'm not going either," Julie announced.

"*I* think it sounds like fun!" Sarah said. "I'll go. We can't let free tickets go to waste. But I don't want to go alone. I haven't driven much in that part of town. Who'll go with me?"

"Count me in," Darby said.

"If Darby is going, I'll go," Jake Saunders piped. He was one of the best-looking guys in Brentwood, and no one—especially Darby—had missed that fact.

"I suppose I should go too," Molly Ashton said. "One way to get into Hollywood is to be discovered on stage. Maybe I'll decide to start out as a stage actress." Molly's future plan was to be a model or movie star. It was, in fact, the main reason she'd signed up for the television production class. She was eager to learn whatever she could about what she referred to as "the business."

"You're going?" Andrew Tremaine looked dismayed. He'd been trying to get on Molly's good side for a long time. It was apparent in his expression that if he *did* volunteer to attend the theater, it would be for only one reason—to be closer to Molly.

At that moment, *Live's!* advisor, Rosie Wright, breezed into the room in a cloud of perfume and chalk dust. She was wearing a gauzy one-piece dress that looked very much like a small, belted tent. Huge brass earrings hung to her shoulders, and her brown hair swung in a braid. "Well, have you decided yet?" she asked abruptly.

"Decided what?"

"Who's going to the theater. I just talked to Gary Richmond and he said he'd like to go if there are still tickets available." Gary, Ms. Wright's assistant and resident cameraman, was as unique and unorthodox as Rosie.

"So far it's Sarah, Darby, Molly, Jake, and Andrew."

"And us," Kate and Julie chimed.

Everyone in the room stared at them. Julie shrugged helplessly, "What's a little old rat compared to a party? If everyone else is going, we want to go too."

"Izzy, Josh, does that include you?" Ms. Wright skewered the pair with a look.

Josh's black curly head bobbed.

Izzy groaned. "I'm not very cultural, Ms. Wright. Last time I tried something 'edifying,' they had to close the museum."

"What does 'edifying' mean? That you ate the museum?" Andrew looked annoyed, as he often did when Izzy used words unfamiliar to his vocabulary.

Though Izzy often *looked* as rumpled as a pile of unfolded clothes on an unmade bed and about as intelligent as cauliflower, under that thick skull and buzz-cut hair, he housed the IQ of a genius.

"Edifying: uplifting, educational, enlightening, instructional," Izzy recited.

"Thank you, Mr. Webster," Andrew sneered. "I knew that all along. I just didn't think *you* knew it."

"Yeah, right."

"You'd better tell us *why* they closed the museum, Isador." Ms. Wright looked both amused and dismayed. Izzy had an unfortunate way of unintentionally causing disruptions which could lead to the closing of large, important buildings.

"Just a little something with the lighting system and the elevator. I was curious to see how it was all wired. How was I supposed to know it was that easy to trip the switches? Some electrical engineer made a really poor mistake . . . ."

"Perhaps Gary *should* go with you." Ms. Wright looked understandably worried. She turned to the silent and aloof member of the team sitting near the window. "Shane? How about you?"

"No way. I'm not the theater type. Besides, I'm going to do some editing. Let someone else go." A familiar sullen expression settled on Shane's features that signaled to everyone in the room that he would not attend the play.

The fact that Shane was even *in* the production class was something of a minor miracle according to those who knew him. Restless, brooding, and occasionally on the fringe of trouble, Shane was hard to get to know and even harder to befriend. He'd developed aloofness to an art form. Still, more than once, it had been Shane who'd given the group direction for their investigative news reports. "Street smart" was the best way to describe him.

He raked his fingers through his straight, dark blond hair. "Just watch out where you park downtown. Use one of the public lots and get under a street light if you can. There are some bad kids hanging out down there."

No one questioned him. Shane had grown up without a father in his life and too little parental monitoring. There'd probably been a time when *he'd* been one of the bad kids hanging out in the uptown area.

"Oh no!" Izzy catapulted out of his chair in front of the graphics generator. "It forgot to watch the time! I have to get to Home Living class. We're finishing our unit on Italian cooking today and we're doing a special red sauce for the spaghetti." An expression of bliss settled across his features. "Fresh tomatoes, garlic, onion . . . it's going to be great. Great? Grate! I'm in charge of the fresh Parmesan. I have to get it grated before class."

"The only reason you even enrolled in Home Living was so you could eat the food," Andrew sneered. "The school food budget has probably gone up ten percent since you started that class."

Izzy didn't make any denials or explanations. Instead he allowed a brief smile to grace his quirky features. "It's my favorite class. Where else could you get easy A's and great food at the same time?"

"As if that's a big concern to you," Darby chastised. "You're an honors student. You could be taking all advanced classes!"

"I'm taking enough of them," Izzy said. "The food . . . I mean, Home Living is a good break in the day."

"He's bright enough to take advanced chemistry and physics," Kate pointed out. "But what does he make a big deal about getting? A spot in the kitchen. Great foresight, Izzy. You'll make some woman a wonderful wife."

"You won't cook all year, will you?" Darby asked. "There must be *other* units. Do you have to sew?"

Izzy looked startled, as though he hadn't considered the possibility that he might have to learn to do something other than cook. "Maybe. It doesn't matter. The teacher's pretty cool. I like the class. Besides, there's nothing about a Home Living class that could be too hard for me, right? What could be so bad?" He glanced at the clock. "Gotta go. Otherwise I might miss the salad. See you later."

"Someday Izzy is going to outsmart himself," Sarah predicted with a mischievous smirk.

---

Izzy *does* outsmart himself—with hilarious results. Ask for *Sarah's Dilemma* at your local bookstore.

## *Live!* From Brentwood High

1 ▪ Risky Assignment
2 ▪ Price of Silence
3 ▪ Double Danger
4 ▪ Sarah's Dilemma

## Other Books by Judy Baer

- Paige
- Adrienne
- Dear Judy, What's It Like at Your House?
- Dear Judy, Did You Ever Like a Boy (who didn't like you?)